THE LEY BETWEEN US

The Ley Between Us

JENNIE ELAINE

The Ley Between Us is a work of fiction. Names, characters, places, and incidents are products of the author's imagination and/or fictitious. Any resemblance to actual persons (living or dead), events, or locales is entirely coincidental.

Published by Ink & Quill Press, 2025
For more excellent works of fiction, visit Inkandquillpress.com

DEDICATION

For those who fill their hearts with romance and magic.
And for Jan and Jenessa, my two biggest fans and creative
partners.

CONTENTS

~ Chapter One ~

WITCH

The seasons had changed twice now and her horrid, hollow heart still cried for her shackles and cage. Night was the worst of it, no darkness ever quite as encompassing as the cell she'd rotted away in. Every dawn brought a different kind of torture—guilt.

Not guilt for the blood of the king's men she'd spilled during her escape, nor for the ways she'd tested and defiled her magic in the name of survival.

No, each day she awoke in a new place, a tree or hollow she'd claimed late the night before, the day already well past high sun, and she'd turn her face to see the grand castle and city she'd fled just over the way. Then guilt would rise like bile, knowing she'd yet to run far enough away.

It had been two seasons since she'd slaughtered her way out of the king's dungeons.

Yet she was still here.

The witch couldn't sleep unless the castle was in sight. The skin of her arms had turned a deep indigo up past her elbows, stained by the magic she'd used to take lives. Her fingers were longer now, foreign to the girl they'd captured years before and yet as much a part of her now as the breath in her chest and the wild raven hair she could never tame.

She held one hand up to her face, parting her fingers until the castle sat betwixt them far in the distance.

She was a wild witch now. A beast her caravan had whispered about around late bonfires to scare their children. Monsters self-made and driven mad by abuse of their Ley-given gifts, or sometimes from the absence of it.

She didn't feel like a monster now, though.

She felt lost.

Worse, she felt tethered to the place and the man sitting on a throne that she would burn beneath him if she ever got the chance.

Two seasons of waking and wishing she could put it all behind her, and today was another day she knew she wouldn't.

Perhaps tomorrow would be easier.

The witch pushed off the tree, jumping to the ground with the grace inherent to her kind, and landed among the fallen leaves. Running her tongue absently behind the elongated canines her magic had also transformed, she considered how she'd spend her time..

Another day wandering lost. Feeding. Bathing. Eating. Keeping her back to the capital city of men until so late in the darkness she couldn't keep her eyes open. Then she'd find another crag or tree where she could stare at the castle walls like a wistful lover and dream of the rats in her prison and the crook in the wall she used to curl against.

Then, she'd sleep.

And begin again.

~ Chapter Two ~

PRINCE

Men were not meant to wander the deep woods here, something that benefited her greatly. They preferred their trails and hunting grounds bathed in light and familiarity. It was not often that foolish or desperate hunters craved the challenge the wild would offer.

It made her solitude easy. She also preferred the familiar markings of these mountainous woods, the quiet reprieve she refused to call home. It was only a way point, she lied to herself, a stepping stone to gather her wits beneath her again and then she would travel onward. Where to, she did not know.

She scented it in the early afternoon. The tang of man and their contraptions, steel that tasted like emptiness on her tongue.

Poachers, or at least one of their traps, no doubt. She took a step towards the scent, her ears pricking at the sound of an animal's cries.

Painful memories of metal bars hit her like a hammer, and she was moving through the trees against her better instincts. She knew what it was to have the magic of the Ley torn from your senses by the cold bite of steel, and she would not let another creature suffer through it.

Even if she craved it nightly.

The witch followed her senses to a small clearing, wide enough for two people to lie across with room to spare. Just within the edge was a contraption of metal and wood designed to ensnare any hapless creature who stepped upon it. Caught beneath its jaw was what first looked to be a fox, until she saw the edges of its dark fur begin to blur. Wild violet eyes, the same color as hers, were wide in fear and pain when it tried to morph out of its current skin and into something better equipped to flee, but the steel prevented it.

A changeling, and a juvenile based on size. She hadn't seen many during her stay in the woods as they were rare, long-lived, and tended to avoid men and monsters alike.

With the indigo stains on her arms, none had ever dared get close.

She dropped into a kind of crouch, the deep blue cloak she wore as her only clothing pooling at her feet. The witch held her hands up to the creature, who now had noticed her at last and shrank from her approach, ears turned downward.

"It's alright, little one," she crooned softly, barely a whisper on the wind. "I'm here to help."

Of that, the changeling wasn't so sure. She kept her attention on it fully, taking her time to whisper and coax it while she drew ever closer. Her knees complained from how long she held her position, her thighs shaking and pained, yet she knew it was a fool's errand to stick her hand in the face of a scared animal, and these things took time.

If someone tried it on *her*, she couldn't promise she wouldn't bite in fear herself.

Slowly, the changeling hid its teeth, its ears rising. The witch kept her hands out, taking things one stooped-over step at a time and beginning the process of trust every time she shortened the distance all over again.

It was no small while later that she made it to the changeling's side, and began to reach for the spring release. The fox-like creature barked and whined, but no longer growled in threat. Taking a moment more to study the trap she leaned in, held down a lever, and released it.

The changeling stepped away from her, but before it could bolt for the woods it was on its side again, whimpering in pain. The leg that had been caught was bleeding a strange iridescent blood, and where it did not *appear* broken, she didn't claim to have the slightest inkling of how steel could hurt a being of pure magic.

"Let me see," she whispered, and to her surprise the creature let her. Her hands touched coarse volpine fur, brushing through the spot to look for any signs something further was wrong. No sooner had she begun her examination than a branch snapped across the clearing.

On instinct she drew the changeling to her chest, holding it close and away from whatever had come to find them. Her eyes shot to the sound, glowing with magic she tried to pull from the ground on instinct, then failing. A human stood on the far side of the clearing, his face red from a long trek, eyes trained on them both.

A growl rose from the changeling's throat, and she was inclined to agree.

The young man was taller than her, but not overly so. He resided somewhere in those early years past teenhood, although he appeared younger than her still. He was solid, with the musculature of a swordsman without the bulk of a warrior. He was tanned from time outdoors with eyes as green as a spring tree and hair a warm honey blonde. It was short shorn, longer on the top and freshly trimmed, curling around his ears with sweat.

She knew that hair. She'd know it anywhere, even if the boy it was attached to was a stranger.

The witch rose to her full height, a graceful, threatening movement not hindered by the creature that clung to her chest. "Blood of the king," she spat the word *king* like a curse, "are you the one who set this trap?"

Her free hand flexed, the temptation to call upon the Ley again strong, in spite of her previous crimes against it. She was shocked at how easy her voice came to her after months of disuse.

The witch may as well have been a domesticated house cat for all the fear he showed at her display, which was to say none at all. It irritated her.

"Far from it," he spoke with a lord's inflection, his voice smooth and calm, "I was dispatched to these woods with a few men to hunt down and stop the poachers bringing beings of magic into our city. I'm pleased to report we accomplished that earlier this morning, and I've had the absolute pleasure of hiking all around the brush for hours collecting their leftovers."

In show, he shifted the pack over one shoulder, the sound of steel and wood clanking heavily within.

"An easy lie," she stepped sideways, prompting him to step opposite and keep her in his line of sight. Not fearful, then, but not so stupid as to let a predator around to his blind spot.

"An easier truth," he countered, nodding to the snare at her feet. "If you'll let me collect that, I only have three more to hunt down. I would prefer to make it home before dark—I haven't had dinner and it's a powerful motivator. That, and the bugs. They're everywhere out here and eating me alive."

Her fingers twitched again. She eyed the sword on his hip, and the hand he kept relaxed on its hilt. A plain scabbard, for a royal. Practical. As was his outfit— dark trousers, well-used boots, and a long sleeved tunic pushed up to his elbows. The changeling in her arms wiggled and whined, drawing her attention for only a moment.

If he'd been talking to keep her distracted and bide him time for an attack, he didn't use it. His hand hadn't moved from the hilt when she turned back to him.

His head was now tilted the opposite direction, much like a dog's would. Studying her. His eyes were quizzical and as bright as a child's seeing their first snow.

"I have no need for steel," she sneered.

"Neither do I, but we can't always get the glamorous jobs." He blinked at her. "Do all witches wander the forest naked? You *are* a witch, I assume. There's magic about you, it's making my nose itch."

Is this human defective? She wondered to herself, *or is he really here for the snare?* He didn't have the air of a poacher. More of a lost pup.

She took another step. He followed. What stood out to her as she shifted fully downwind was the lack of blood on his scent. A poacher would have the tang of magic and fear soaked into his clothes. This boy did not. And once he was carried on the breeze to the changeling it relaxed, a sign he was not a threat.

"Which son are you?" She asked instead, narrowing her eyes at him. "Give me your name."

"Rorian Delafoy," he answered, "the youngest."

That fits. She had never been graced with any siblings, but a lifetime ago she'd been a part of a larger family. A commune that traveled together, taught each other the art of magic and shared in food and company. She'd known friends from larger families well enough to recognize the symptoms of being the youngest sibling. Childish, even as an adult. Coddled.

"Do *you* have a name?" He asked, moving opposite her again as she took another step around the clearing.

"Not one for the likes of men," she all but snarled. The prince, to her unending frustration, did not flinch away. Only tilted his head even further.

"Then it's true, that the names of magical beings hold power?"

Yes, and no. But that was not a nuance she was going to spell out for him.

"Think what you will," she dismissed the conversation instead. She was not in the mood to lengthen the stain on her skin over a worthless pup like him. "And take what you want. Do not return to this forest once your work is done."

"I can have the snare, then?"

"I said I had no use for steel."

The changeling in her arms whimpered in pain. What she needed was somewhere quiet to look it over and properly tend to any wounds.

"Go," she ordered, "and do not return." she began to step back, meaning to slip between the treeline.

"Will you be here tomorrow?" He called out to her retreating form.

"No," she lied, and left the boy standing alone.

In a show of wisdom, he did not follow.

~ Chapter Three ~

DIVE

The changeling had left her by dawn, well enough to leave on its own. Fair enough, she reasoned, she was miserable company to anyone these days.

The smell of steel and blood still clung to her cloak and skin, an unpleasant mixture that brought forth even more unpleasant memories. Her day was decided the moment she dropped from that night's tree, heading for her favorite lake. A nice bath would wash away the scent and memories, and give her time to forget the strange man who had intruded on her lands. Yes, she decided, setting forth, that's exactly what she needed.

It was barely ten minutes into her swim that her day was ruined. No twigs were snapped this time, but she was downwind from his approach.

She ignored him long enough, keeping her back to him while deciding if she even *could* pull the Ley to her if needed, and gave up. Avoidance clearly would not work here.

"Little Prince," crooned The witch, "I can scent you."

"I'm not exactly trying to hide," came Rorian's amused chuckle. "You're the one who's kept your back to me. I've left myself in plain sight on the bank."

She turned to see him and, indeed, he was far from hidden. Today he was in a simple linen tunic, unlaced at the top, with a leather traveling jacket against the breeze and the same dark pants tucked into the same boots. She could smell the steel from yesterday still clinging to the threads, and his sweat from the hike.

He was standing on the wet silt of the bank, his boots sinking in, his arms crossed, his head tilted again as he studied her. Again, she got the feeling that he was not staring at her as a woman, but as a curious animal he'd only just discovered.

Somehow, that irked her worse than the lecherous look of a man. At least *that* she knew how to handle.

In challenge, she stood to her full height, letting the water run down her body. He took her in, from her full breasts to her lean, muscled form. She was thinner than she should be, she knew, but not meek. Months in the wilds had strengthened her feeble body, but without a properly balanced diet she'd not had the chance to bulk.

"What do you see," she found herself asking, sneering at his curiosity, "a beast that looks like a woman? Or only a monster?"

"Well," he leaned forward, as if to get a closer look despite the distance between them, "I'm afraid I can't answer that."

Irritation ticked her brow. "And why is that?"

"Because those options are so limited." He put his hands in his trouser pockets, tilting his head the other way to study her. "To start, I could never see anyone who would be so caring towards another life as a monster."

He meant the changeling from the day before. "So I'm a beast who looks like a woman."

"I never said that."

"Those were your options. You said I'm not a monster."

"I'm choosing another option." He leaned forward, unlacing one of his boots and tugging it off.

"What are you doing?"

"Joining you, if you'll allow it," he began on the second boot, nearly tripping over himself to accomplish it.

"I don't allow it."

"And why not?" Next came the tunic, tossed over the same log as his jacket. He, blissfully, left his trousers on. "Unless you're planning to drown me? I've heard tales of witches dragging unsuspecting young men to their graves at the bottom of the sea."

"Those are sirens, not witches," she said with more than a huff of annoyance. She had not moved to cover herself, now instead putting her hands on her hips to show him her displeasure.

"So you won't drown me?"

"I didn't promise that."

"I've gambled on worse odds," he waded into the water up to his ankles, hissing in a breath. "Oh *hells,* this is cold."

She took a few steps deeper, keeping distance between her and this strange royal fool. "And how did that work out for you?"

"Terribly," he laughed, a pleasant and genuine sound. "I've lost more than a pretty copper at cards before."

"Do you have *no* sense of self preservation?" She nearly barked at him, bewildered at this whole situation and with half a mind to flee. Or actually drown him, although that came with its own risks. Namely, attracting unwanted humans to her territory.

"I'm beginning to think that no, I do not." Rorian waded in up to his chest, letting her maintain a healthy distance from him. This close she could see old scars from swords on his body, light cuts from sparring matches or lucky escapes. It was only then that she realized he was without a sword that day.

He made a show of holding his breath, puffing his cheeks out with air and plugging his nose before submerging fully. In a matter of moments, he was surfaced again, gasping for breath and pushing back his wet hair. "Do you know what I see you as?"

"I don't care to know anymore," she said curtly, sinking into the water up to her shoulders.

"I see you as a good conversationalist, a...kind soul, and, apparently, a nudist."

"I haven't spoken to anyone in seasons," she snarked back, "I was long stripped of any care for sensibility and live alone regardless, and you do not earn *these* by being a *kind soul*."

She lifted her arms above the water, showing him her indigo hands and elongated nails. The prince swam closer as if to study them, that damnable spark of curiosity in his eyes. She dropped her hands back underwater as quickly as she'd raised them.

"So it's *not* ink," he mused, stopping his advancement. "I wondered yesterday where you would find such a rich tone in these woods."

"It's not," she snapped, harsher than she'd meant to. *Why was she entertaining him?*

"Well," he pressed, "what is it, then?"

Now *that* was not a question she planned to answer.

"Have you picked up a habit of stalking me or do you truly have a death wish?"

"Perhaps," Rorian said, his voice surprisingly raw, "I'm lonely."

She sputtered. Damn near *laughed*. Now *that* was a long-forgotten sound. "Then get a dog."

"I have dogs. They are not good conversationalists."

"Oh," she swam around him, watching him follow her movements, "I think you're a conversationalist enough for both of you."

"Is it so hard to believe that I'm captivated by you?" He turned with her, his eyes a sparkling green in the water's reflection. "That I found you *beyond* fascinating yesterday, tossed and turned all night unable to forget our encounter and cleared my schedule to run away and trek all over these damned woods for a chance at finding you again today?"

"I'm not interested."

"In what?"

"In *you*," she said, stopping in a place where her feet didn't touch and she had to tread water. "In your loneliness *or* your conversation."

"Because of my blood?" He raised his eyebrows, remembering some of her first words to him

"If your blood was the issue here," she said lowly, not hiding the power that rose to meet her fingertips and danced across her skin, "you would have died yesterday."

"You've made it clear that you don't care for the royal family," he said plainly, "why?"

Flashes of her cell came back to her. Her captivity. The deaths of everyone she'd ever known at the hands of the true monster in power.

"If you want to know that," she told him, "visit the lowest floor of the western wing of your father's castle. Find the stairs that take you deeper. Bother someone else for answers. I'm done with you, Little Prince."

And with that, she dipped below the surface, swimming down deeper than she knew he would dare and laying on the bottom of the lake bed. Alone.

~ Chapter Four ~

FLAMES

When she emerged again, it was long after dark. Holding her breath for so long was quite an act of meditation without the ease of full magical abilities, yet she'd managed. Even napped for a while.

She rose silently from the surface of the lake to a deep black sky with only the faintest sliver of moon. But where the forest should have been dark, it was bright with the flickering orange glow of flames.

A small bonfire, to be specific. Her eyes were drawn to the bank where the prince had appeared that afternoon, finding a lone shape sitting beside the source of light.

It's not too late to drown him, she reasoned.

The witch walked out of the rippling water onto the bank, keeping to his blind spot. The scent of freshly charred meat wrapped around her senses, wetting her tongue and tightening her empty stomach.

"You're still here," she approached on silent feet, stepping into the warmth. Rorian turned to her, a tight smile on his expression.

"I left, for a while," he admitted, "a friend told me to seek answers at the lowest floor of my father's western wing."

"I am *not* a friend," she stood there, letting the fire dry her dripping skin, hands returning to her hips.

"Even so," he allowed her, less of his normal joking tone in his words, "the information was good."

The witch studied him, noting the tight line of his lips and dark circles of stress beneath his eyes, then settled on a log he'd pulled beside the flame. The tattered cloak she'd washed hours before was now dry and folded across it. Her eyes shimmered an unnatural violet in the light, the mark of her magic.

"What did you find?" She asked in kind.

The prince was quiet for long moments, turning a stick over the flame with an impressive slab of meat skewered on it. A pig of some kind, from the scent. Flavored with herbs you couldn't find in these woods.

"It was hidden," he began. "In my lifetime growing up in those walls, I've never heard of the sub basement, nor could I have guessed its purpose or necessity. The door was stone perfectly masked to the wall around it. I only discovered it from a light draft when I pressed my hands to the crack. There were no wall sconces beyond, no place for lights to be set at all. The air was cold, and stale, and stank of rot and musk. Worse, the further I descended."

She set her hands back on the log, crossing her legs while he spoke and listened with a pained curiosity about her last home.

"The walls were carved out, none of the cells higher than my shoulder. Imported steel from the south was used to bar the cells, a ward against magic if the stories I've heard are to be true."

"They are," she gave him. "The Ley does not flow through the metals of men."

"The Ley…" he turned the word over on his tongue, tilting his head again. "I've heard about it in books. The magic of the earth, is it not?"

"More," was all she gave. "What else did you find?"

"The cells were empty," she was not surprised, "long abandoned. The further in I went the more the walls turned black. I touched them, and dark ash came away, like someone smeared it there and left it unclean."

Her mind snapped her back to the day she'd escaped, the screams of the Ley in her ears, the twisted magic she pulled to her fingers and unleashed on any man who dared to come near. What they'd turned into when she'd ripped the very life from them.

"It was cold, harsh. I've seen cells before but these… it wasn't humane." He stopped turning the spit, staring into the flickering flames. "It didn't feel like my home. It felt like the place souls go to rot. But there were no guards there, and no one I could ask, so," he tilted his eyes to hers, his voice small. "I came back to you."

The fire popped, the only sound between them. Her stomach was tight with memories, and a hunger so deep it carved into her with claws.

"A trade," she said at last, her voice barely loud enough to carry to him, "information, if you'll share your meal."

His eyes were alight again, the prince nodding his acceptance to her deal. In no time at all the meat was removed from the flame, cut with a small blade from his boot— one he'd had the grace to clean beforehand— and served to her on a bark slab. It was the fullest meal she'd faced in months, and the first shared with another since before her imprisonment.

She stilled at the thought, allowing her mind to drift to nights around bonfires just like this, her mother dancing under the moon and the flavor of her father's…expressive cooking. Overseasoned was a better word. She couldn't remember his laugh anymore, but she could still feel its echo booming in her chest as it had when she was a child.

She picked at the meat, cooled a piece with her breath, then began to chew.

It was utterly delicious.

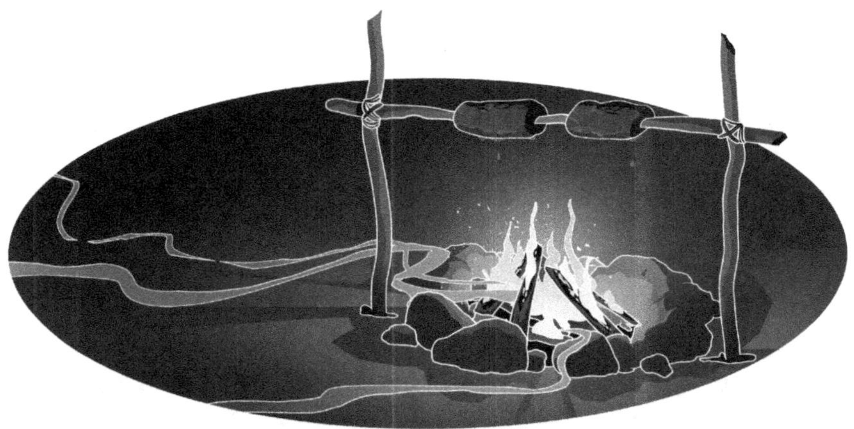

The prince watched her eat a few more bites, then began on his own. She was in no rush to tell this tale, nor had she promised when she'd begin. Rorian, to his credit, let her take the time to gather her thoughts.

"I was eighteen when your father came to our caravan," she began, "barely a woman. For his efforts my family was killed and I and one more younger girl were brought to the castle. To those cells."

The prince was no longer eating, a piece of meat halfway to his mouth. She continued.

"The cells were never tall enough to let us stand. She and I were separated, placed on opposite ends of the line. We were not the only ones there."

Once, those cells had been full. The smell of must and sick and fear overwhelming her senses. She put another piece of pork in her mouth, taking the time to enjoy the favor and let it override her memories.

"Why keep you down there?" The prince asked, his eyes serious. He leaned his body towards her, listening to her every word.

"Steel," she said, spitting out the word. "They wanted to see how steel would affect witches in its many forms. Powder in our food. Weapons, impaling anyone who fought against them, rods inserted through cuts in the skin and left to fester. The bars that held us and the drivel they called food kept us weak, easier to control."

The flame roared on a soft wind, fueling the fire higher into the night. "I lasted the longest."

"The girl you came with?" He sounded hopeful for an answer she did not have.

"Beheaded," the witch turned her eyes to the moon. "She didn't last the first month. Tried to escape at every chance while her strength was still there. She was young, a child, hadn't even had her first bleed. She was a fighter who refused to see herself become a cornered animal under the boots of men."

"Yet you're here," he set aside the last of his food, unable to continue with his stomach in knots. "How did you make it out?"

The witch did not answer for long heartbeats. The moon was nearly full that night, waning sliver by sliver into a new moon a few weeks away.

"The business of murder is the prerogative of men," she spoke to the moon, and then, to the prince she said "taking a life with magic is against every natural order. And it was a line I would not cross. I took everything your king's men gave me— the wounds, the starvation—for *years*. Time held no meaning, I counted the months first by the days, then by my bleeds, and then when those stopped...I lost track. I slept curled against the corner and spoke only to the rats that refused scraps of my food. The men found me boring, my results not to their care, and they preferred the ones that put up a fight. I never learned how to fight," she took out a long breath, her eyes turning to the deep indigo her arms had become, "but those men taught me how to kill. Then, one day, they left my cage unlocked. Turned their backs on me. And I showed them in kind."

Her voice was a deep, dreadful thing. For the first time since Rorian had met her he felt the hair on the back of his neck rise in warning, instinct screaming of the danger that sat across from him. She was, if only for a brief moment, not the curious thing that had spent a long half hour earning the trust of an injured animal to set it free. She *was* that injured animal, trapped in the moment she'd turned on the men foolish enough to keep her in a cage.

Rorian swallowed. Her eyes flicked to his neck, aware of his nerves.

"You escaped." He surmised.

"Yes," she allowed him, tearing her eyes away at last to finish her meal, "and I took them all with me."

"How many?"

"Twelve," she answered, "and one out of mercy. Another witch on the brink of starvation. True starvation, where the muscles have atrophied enough everything begins to shut down. The men had found their answers, and started to bring in less and less of us over time. They were set to eliminate us both and move on to other cruelties."

Horror flooded his blood. "The steel swords," he said.

"Beheading is most effective. We are not so...adverse to steel in our systems as magical beings, for we are *not* magical beings but beings of magic." She tore into the last of her meat with her teeth, dropping the wooden slat into the fire. "But that did not stop them from trying everything else, first. They found what weakened us through the blood of me and my kin, and once they had their answers, they went to toss us aside. To end our lives and move on. I only relieved them of that duty first."

The fire danced, licking up the offering of fresh wood. "Why stay here, then?" He asked, and for that...she did not have an answer.

"Does it matter?" She answered with a question instead.

"Could you guess at how long you were there?"

She ran a hand between her breasts. "Long enough to grow from a young woman into a woman. Beyond that, I couldn't say."

His eyes followed that hand, then quickly found her face once more. "How long have you been free?"

She felt... almost embarrassed to admit it. Then her old friend guilt rose to the surface. Guilt for living, guilt for staying. Guilt for not being stronger sooner, for doing what needed done.

"Two seasons, now." It was a surprise to offer him the truth. Perhaps she had spent too long alone with these thoughts in her head.

He nodded, looking at her arms. "You said you earned that stain, what did you mean?"

She breathed in, and out again, deciding her words. She'd already told him this much.

"Magic is not for death," she explained, looking down at the color in her palms. "It is for life, and giving. To kill with it...magic does not forget. To twist it as such, it mars you. Corrupts you from within. Turns you wild, beastly, incapable of thought yet trapped in your own repentance until death comes for you, usually at the end of a sword."

"A wild witch," he guessed.

He handed her the last morsels of his food, no longer in the mood. She accepted it, not sure where her next good meal might come.

"This is...far from what I've always been told." He ran his hands over his face, exhaling to steady his nerves. "Yet, it must be true. You are here, in front of me, I saw the cages, and you are not a liar."

"Witches rarely are," she said, "we do not waste breath with falsities."

"Yet humans are full of them." He leaned back, turning his eyes to the stars, mulling everything over. "I've grown up in a royal court. Life is a series of lies and treachery there, everyone crawling over each other to gain favor and status. Only the king's word is law."

"Law is not truth," she finished half of the offered meat in one bite.

"So it seems." Rorian's face was illuminated by the flames, his jawline sharpened with dark shadows, his hair as bright as the finest gold. "My father's crusade against your kind is fueled by fear. My brothers lead men to face that fear every day. It was a witch who killed our mother, took the very life from her with his magic and turned towards the crown. I lost her young, but not so young that I do not feel her absence or know my father's pain."

"This witch was either a fool or a cover," she spelled out for him, finishing this meal as well and repeating her toss of the wood perfectly, landing it on top of the blackened remains of the first.

"Men are always looking for excuses to hurt us. To go against the royalty of your kind is to guarantee death and invite this very *crusade*, as you've called it. We are not a foolish people; we are survivors, the hands of the earth. We do not care for your titles or power. The power of men is false and fleeting before the Ley."

"As *I've* called it," he picked out of her words. "What would you call it, then?"

That was the easiest question to answer all night. "Genocide," she gave him.

The fire spoke for them for long minutes. The prince swallowed her words, turned to the flames for answers, then the sky, and at last, her.

"This... staining," he motioned to her hands. "Is there a way to avoid it? If you kill with magic, I mean. A way to cheat the system."

"No." She had not moved while he thought, and now did not avoid his eyes. "A question for you now, little prince. This witch that killed your mother with magic... what color were his hands?"

Rorian didn't answer. He didn't need to. She already knew.

The witch stood, gathering her tattered cloak from the seat.

"The King's word is law," she reminded him, "but law is not the truth. Thank you for the meal."

She turned to leave him.

"Wait," he called after her, halting her in her tracks, her back to him, the cloak across her shoulders. "I still don't know your name."

"I told you," she continued to walk away, "my name is not for the likes of men."

She left the prince by his fire and stepped back into the woods, running from this conversation and the strange man she'd stayed to have it with.

Chapter Five

HEARTLESS

The witch sent a prayer to the Ley that night that the impossible man would find his way home and stay there, leaving her to her woods and solitude. The Ley, as it had done since her night twisting it to take a life, ignored her.

Her prayers fell on deaf ears.

Three weeks had passed since that night, and she barely went more than a few days before the prince would find her again. He had a keen sense for tracking her down, much to her annoyance, even as she started to avoid the places he'd found her before.

Rorian was filled with questions up to his ears, it seemed. Their visits were flooded with his constant curiosity, be it about magic, or her, or her life in the woods. She avoided answering him at every possible chance, only entertaining him as repayment for the times he brought her food, and bring her food he did.

The prince must have drained the kitchens dry of their stores, for she'd had her fill of rich breads and cheeses, spiced meats he often cooked himself, and, on occasion, a rare sugary treat he saved for her. She was never one for sweet delicacies, but flavor was a luxury in her life in the wild and she accepted them nonetheless.

"How old are you?" He asked one day while leaning against a tree, watching her devour a pastry that tasted both sour and sweet with a whipped frosting on top. "Guess, if you have to."

"Older every minute you pester me with questions," she'd answered in annoyance.

She'd just woken barely an hour before, and could still see the tree she'd slept in for all the distance she'd gotten before he'd found her.

"I've passed my twenty-first summer," he surprised her. "My twenty-second is next season."

"Yet you act like a child." He laughed as if she'd delivered a particularly funny joke, a nice, booming sound that filled the woods between them.

"So my brothers say. I'm the youngest by a few years. My eldest has nearly a decade over me."

Mikaeus Delafoy, the crown prince. She'd learned his name long before she came to the dungeons.

"I am younger than him," she gave, "yet older than you."

"That's a relief," she gave him a hard quizzical look. He put his hands up. "I didn't know how long witches lived, for all I knew you had centuries above me."

"I do in wisdom," she'd replied, licking her fingers free of the frosting.

That earned her another laugh. "That you do. Tell me, is it true witches eat babies?"

She'd thrown dirt at him for that.

Another time she'd been washing her cloak in a small stream, having avoided the lake he'd first found her at, in hopes that it would give her peace. It did not.

"You speak very formally," he turned his head like a pup again, a motion she'd grown accustomed to.

He was sitting on a large boulder sticking up from the slow-moving water, his boots removed and trousers pushed up—not rolled, he rarely took the time—to dip his feet in.

"Do you have nothing to do as a prince?" She'd grumbled, rubbing the cloth over a porous rock to release dirt from the hem.

"Oh, plenty," he'd told her. "But I'm good at finishing my work and finding time for you."

"Time I did not ask for."

"This week," he ignored her, "a cousin came to visit with his two young daughters. One of my father's advisors has a son in need of a second wife—the first one passed in childbirth last year, a true tragedy, but then again he'd married her *far* too young. Always had this...taste for younger fare."

He made a face of disgust that told her enough on his personal regard for the man's taste.

"My cousin is desperate to arrange a marriage for his daughters, as it's no secret he's deeply in debt after too many failings as a merchant. Lost another ship to the sea last winter in spite of our counsel to sail around the western pass instead of through it...again. Regardless, my father's advisor is known for his financial prosperity, and so my cousin wormed his way into a dinner affair to try and talk up his daughters in this man's favor. They're twins, barely past their tenth year."

"Only past their tenth year?" She found herself getting sucked into his story by shock value alone.

He nodded, his eyes bright. "Exactly! My cousin is a fool, they're far too young for such an agreement. Longer engagements aren't unheard of in my world, promised young and married as adults, but my cousin knew of the advisor's son's tastes and was actually *hoping* to secure a wedding within the year to pay off his debts."

"What a worm," she turned back to her work.

"A far nicer word than I had used. Regardless, I was ordered to sit between them and find a favorable outcome for all. I'm sure it was meant to help pave the path for such an agreement, but I could never broker such a deal."

"What happened?" She asked, one of the first times she'd engaged him in such a way.

The prince groaned, rubbing his face. Another quirk she'd grown used to. "It was one of the longest dinners of my life, but luck was on my side, as I'd been given advance notice about the situation. My middle brother, Jordan, had headed off my cousin upon his arrival and warned me of his intent. So I'd had time to plan."

"Your brother did not approve of this deal?"

Rorian snorted. "Jordan? Oh no. He's a good man, one of the best, and isn't afraid to call my cousin far worse than a worm to his face when given the chance. Which isn't often, so he didn't waste it this time. Jordan's not really one for politics—he's better with a sword, which is why he's a general and I have to sit through long dinners and prevent some poor ten-year-old from cruel fates such as this."

"Did you manage it?"

"Barely. I knew of another courtier with a son much closer to their age and invited him to the dinner last minute. He's never quite been in perfect standing with my father, far too meek to do what needs done to earn true favor and climb over others, but I had him sit opposite us. With enough negotiating he was more than happy to broker a long engagement with a member of the extended royal family and even advance my cousin a hefty business investment, as he needs goods shipped across the sea this summer. I made sure to suggest he pay for his own navigator, though, after the dinner."

"That does sound exhausting." She gave him, pulling her cloak out to begin the wringing process. She stood with water up to her knees, enjoying the late spring day and the warmth on her shoulders.

"Terribly so. But with that out of the way and a favorable nod from my father for my handling of the situation, I secured a day to come here."

"Does your father know what you do out here?" She eyed him with caution.

"I would rather pluck out my eyes than tell my family why I'm here," he answered with a sincerity that shocked her. "No, my mother was fond of nature herself. They've figured I've come to enjoy the outdoors as she had. I told them it helps ground me, evens out my stress. Considering our conversations put me in a much better mood when I return, they have waved on my little expeditions. Plus," he added, "they trust me to take care of myself."

"Yet you never bring a sword." Not the smartest idea this deep in the woods.

"Would you allow me near you if I did?" he challenged.

No, no she would not.

"You are a fool."

"Jordan would agree. Just in harsher words."

"I speak with formality," she answered his far earlier question, wringing the cloak between her hands, "because words are powerful. I was raised to speak clearly as magic is woven in speech, even if we do not intend it."

"So you have to speak to weave spells?" Rorian asked.

"Some do, I do not. But honeyed words are their own kind of magic, are they not? Seduction, lies, manipulation... it is all a game of words as intricate as any spellwork."

Rorian laughed again. "I guess that makes me a witch, then, as that's all I do at home."

"No, little prince," she held up the cloak before her, checking that nothing was missed. "It makes you an annoying little shit."

Rorian laughed so hard at that he fell into the water, and was forced to join her and her cloak sunning on the bank, his shirt laid out to dry.

Over time she grew used to his presence. Tolerated it, even. Rorian became an inevitable part of her life, weaving himself in and out of her days. He told her about affairs in court, about the long weeks waiting for his brothers to return and the quiet without them.

He seemed to think highly of the two older men, but was courteous enough to never spell it out for her on where the two princes went and for why. She could guess, regardless. Witches were still 'kill on sight' in this country, something that had started shortly after her capture.

Rorian was a very bright man, clever and outgoing, easy to speak to. She didn't offer up her full history, and since that first night by the fire he hadn't asked about the cells again. He was quick to laugh and quicker to smile, and found wonder in the woods. In time the witch showed him some of the paths of the natural creatures there, told him lore of magical beings she'd grown up with and ones she'd seen. She learned that he could read and speak in three languages and was still suffering tutors for a fourth. She knew only two, the tongue they conversed in and the silent word of the Ley.

It was another week before she gave up her avoidance of places he'd found her before. She missed the lake she enjoyed bathing in most, and it was one such day he found her again.

Rorian arrived on the banks around midday, not bothering to hide his footfall. Their campfire area was still set up, her cloak draped across one of the logs they'd sat on. Clouds were gathering overhead for a storm, but it was still far off. Perhaps that evening.

She had been floating in the water, enjoying the peace of the lake, until he'd arrived and she'd righted herself to wade back to a depth where her feet could touch.

Rorian was in a leather jacket and his usual attire of tunic, pants, and boots. The spring was lingering cold further into the season than usual. His arrival was upwind so his scent would carry to her, a habit he'd adopted after his questioning of her heightened senses two weeks before. Today he carried a simple pack with him, and from it he produced a few packages of food and another, larger paper bundle wrapped in twine he set on the log beside her cloak.

"Good morning," he called out, knowing she preferred to sleep in late. "Lunch?"

"I could eat," she gave him, heading his way. He made quick work of the fire, pulling out seasoned meat for both of them, bread, and a few fruits she'd never seen.

"A gift from a visiting dignitary," he explained, laying a flat rock over the fire to warm. "I've had them before, they're not as sweet as a pastry, more of a tart flavor. They taste good with the meat."

"Venison?" She sniffed, sitting on a log beside her cloak.

"You're good at that," he gave her, holding a hand over the stone before setting them to sear. "From our woods, butchered last night."

"Does your kitchen know you steal all this?" She asked at last, having wondered for a while now.

"Oh I'm a piss poor thief," he admitted, "they caught me weeks ago. The cook was more annoyed than anything, told me to at least tell him what I wanted to take so he could adjust their inventory. I've asked for everything ever since."

"They don't question that you bring two portions?'

"Way ahead of you there," he promised, taking out a knife to cut the fruit for her. "I've started eating more at dinner to convince them it's all for me."

"A clever little prince," she took a piece of offered green fruit, popping it in her mouth. It was tart as he'd promised. "And soon a fat one, if you keep that up."

"I think all the hiking is taking care of that," he patted his stomach, the sound of hard muscles greeting her. "I also practice swordplay regularly."

"You've thought of everything then," she watched him flip the meat using his knife, the smell like heaven to her.

"A few things," he said, getting their wooden plates ready. He offered her a water bladder for her to drink from, which she accepted, then pulled out his own. He prattled on about the cook some more, and pranks his brothers and him used to get up to in the kitchens. "I'm a lot closer in age to Jordan than Mikaeus," he explained, plating their food. "So we were often getting in trouble as kids together."

"It sounds more like he got you in trouble than the other way around," she surmised.

That earned her another easy laugh. She'd decided that she liked the sound.

"That's fair, he wasn't initially pleased when the title of youngest was taken from him. He grew more fond of me after the horse incident."

"Horse incident?"

"A story for another time," he waved off, handing her the food. "Oh! I also brought you a gift," he motioned to the package next to her on the log.

She eyed it with suspicion. "Isn't the food enough?"

"Just open it," he urged, his eyes bright.

The witch took a few bites of her food first before reaching for the package, savoring the flavor of deer and the fruit together. She had to give Rorian one thing, he was a damn good cook. The paper tore easily under her long dark nails, falling aside when she pulled out a long bundle of thin fabric.

"Try it on," he said.

She stood, holding it up and letting the cloth fall to its full length. It was beautiful, a dark midnight tone with rich blue undertones, made of an expensive and thin fabric for the upcoming summer months. A simple silver clasp in the shape of a moon was the only adornment, the collar long enough to be a hood yet designed to fall in a fashionable way over her shoulders when down.

"A cloak?" She asked, feeling the fabric between her fingers. It smelled like fresh laundering soap.

"Yours is heavier, and getting a little ragged," he admitted, "and you said you don't really care for clothes, so when I spotted it while shopping the other day, well, I uh, I thought of you."

It was the first time she'd heard him stumble over his words, growing quieter and unsure. The strange prince never seemed to fail to surprise her.

She stepped back from the fire, twirling the cloak over her shoulder and letting it settle there, clasping the little moon. It fell to mid calf on her, and the fabric felt absolutely divine on her skin. Cooling instead of smothering warmth like her last one.

Rorian watched her turn in it, unable to look away. The midnight color matched her hair, made it look like a perfect extension of her. Her indigo hands came up to pull up the hood, tucking her hair within. It fit well, draping over her frame in all the right ways. Not for the first time he felt himself looking up and down those curves, but this time he was still staring when she caught him.

Their eyes met, hers in challenge. She was no stranger to that look from men. In the past, she'd even dressed to provoke it.

"You shouldn't lust after monsters," she warned him, "even the tamest of beasts get hungry."

The prince recovered from being caught quickly. "You're welcome to take a bite, if you'd like." He took off his jacket, laying it across a nearby log and rolling up his sleeve for her to see. "It wouldn't be the first time something's managed it."

She recognized the large square scars immediately. "What horse had the displeasure of your presence?" She inquired about the bite mark.

"My father's, years ago." She realized only after he answered that she'd truly cared enough to ask. "Jordan played a trick on me, locking me in with his old war horse."

"Heartless," she recalled the name of the beast. The prince blinked in surprise.

"Yes. You know him?"

"I know horses," she answered. "And there isn't a being in this realm that does not know the name of that monster."

Nor the stories of it racing into battle, eighteen hands high and black as death, the king in his saddle, tearing through anyone who got in their way.

Children and innocents included.

"As I said," he smiled, "I've already had a monster take a nip. I'll survive another, or perhaps I won't and I'll die for playing with fire and catching aflame."

The witch stared at the prince like he was the biggest fool she'd ever met. And, in honesty, he may very well be.

"You survived an encounter with Heartless," she asked instead, "as a child? How?"

The Prince chuckled in memory. "I bit him back."

Well that was... unexpected. The witch took her turn studying the man, appraising him in a new way. "You bit a horse eighteen hands high?"

"Tasted awful." She chuckled at that, the first time laughing for him. He smiled wide, emboldened by this new gift. "I would hope you'd taste better."

"Witches don't eat children," she poked fun at him for a long-ago question, "but we're not above eating stupid princes who offer to *taste* them."

"You're worth the risk."

"I'm really not," she said in dismissal as much as warning.

"Someday," he admitted, "I hope to be the judge of that."

The witch took him in, from the wistful want in his eyes to the way he sat forward, his body turned to hers and not afraid at all in the way it should be, and realized she had two avenues to pursue from here.

One, the *sane* one, was to remind him again why wanting her in that way was a terrible, awful idea and one that would never happen. She was a wild witch forsaken by the Ley and tortured on the order of his father.

The other was...decidedly less in the interest of her ongoing survival. But his cute smile, and terrible jokes, and easy laugh tempted that path all the same.

"Someday," she said, "I will eat you alive."

She let that promise lie where it did, somewhere between the two paths, halfway between a threat and... and a challenge.

Rorian smiled. "Have I earned your name yet?"

"No," she said, taking her seat again on the log and returning to her food, "but keep feeding me this well and perhaps I'll consider it."

The prince chuckled again, turning back to his own meal. "I'll remember that."

~ Chapter Six ~

DOWNPOUR

The skies opened by late evening, and the heavens poured onto the world without mercy. The witch sought cover in a cave she had claimed a while before, one a single leap above the forest floor on the side of a rocky outcropping. A tree overhead had let its roots grow down and around the opening, keeping out most of the wind and rain.

She liked the rain, but when it came down this hard it stifled scents and made it difficult to see any distance. It made traversing the forest dangerous, and she was not stupid enough to risk her life for such a thing. She had nowhere to be, regardless. The prince had left before the skies came down, letting her know he wouldn't be back until at least after the storm had passed.

From how dark the skies were the next morning, she knew that was going to be a while, so she'd settled back into her solitude.. Two days passed in his absence with no sign of the rain relenting.

Sitting alone under cover, she realized that the time without him felt...lonely. She curled up under her new cloak before the small fire she'd set, and wondered if, in the prince's quest to ease his own disquiet life in her presence, he'd shifted the concept unto her in his absence.

I miss him, she confessed to herself and the flames, frowning at this new revelation. Rorian Delafoy was annoying, persistent, and now seemed to have a growing interest in her that couldn't go anywhere good, and yet she no longer yearned for the days before he'd crashed into her life. She'd grown used to having him around, and knowing it would be a while before his return felt different this time. Upsetting.

She stood to pace the small alcove. That was not good. Not good at *all*. It wasn't too late to go back, she hoped, to push him away and return to her life of solitude.

Yet to what end? She wasn't a wanderer like in her youth, traveling with purpose in her family's caravan. She also wasn't stable by any means, her aimless wanderings a far cry from settled. She was stagnant and lost, with nowhere to return to and no path forward. Every day was another survived, but who was she anymore? Not a prisoner, not a daughter. She was nothing. No one.

She was alone.

The rain came harder. The paths risked mudslides now, the waterways flooding. It was the first real rain of the season and it seemed nature meant to make it count.

The sound of tiny feet on stone snapped her eyes to the entrance of her cave, and she attempted to draw magic to her on instinct. It fought her back like being pulled through tar. It seemed the Ley still had not forgiven her. She relaxed only when she saw the small changeling at her door, sodden from the storm in its volpine form.

"Hello little one," she spoke softly, moving slowly to crouch on the balls on her feet, "do you need shelter from the rain?"

The creature mewled, bounding towards her. She wasn't expecting it, unsure of its reasoning. Was it injured? Desperate? Changelings rarely approached anyone, let alone a wild witch. It wasn't until she caught a faint scent in the air that she set rigid.

The changeling dropped something in front of her, mewling again. A small strip of cloth, torn with its teeth. She snatched it from the stone, scenting it close to her nose.

Rorian.

"Where did you get this?" She demanded of the creature, who bounded in anxious circles. "Is he here? In the woods?"

It mewled again, then let out a near bark sound, its edges shimmering like evaporating oil. She stood at once, switching her new cloak for her older, heavier one.

"Show me," she demanded of the creature, and as if it understood it turned and bounded for the entrance, leaving her to follow.

She ran after it.

The rain was unforgiving, her feet sinking heavily in mud as she ran. Again, she begged the Ley for magic to help her steps, and again she felt only the barest slip of magic come to her with a groan. In frustration she stopped trying, slogging through and jumping onto exposed roots wherever possible.

The changeling was an ever-changing form of bird, then fox, then dog, and more, always ahead of her, stopping when need be and looking back with impatience for her to catch up. She offered no apologies, only gritted her teeth and willed her stubborn body to travel faster.

Down a small valley in the way of the castle path they came to another drop. One that hadn't been there the day before. The downpour had pulled mud away from an overflowing riverbed and along with it a cascade of sticks and moderately sized trees. The wood had clogged a natural drainage area and water was rising in the new basin.

The changeling turned back to its fox form, running in circles with yips and barks while she grabbed an upright tree to steady herself and squinted into the din of the downpour.

There, just along the edge of it, stuck in mud up higher than his knees and wrapped weakly around a log stuck upright in the muck, was a sudden patch of familiar honey hair. The witch moved without thought, jumping from log to log to reach him, keeping clear of the mud.

Rorian's eyes looked up as she approached, drawn by the flashing white of the changeling that reached him first.

"You came," he said, seeing her next.

"I should let the flood take you and let you drown with lungs full of mud for your idiocy," she snarled, climbing up to the upturned roots of the tree he clung to and hooking her knees under a sturdy branch.

"Where's the fun in that?" He croaked, not even managing a smile.

He was shivering, soaked to the bone, and had clearly been here long before the changeling found him.

The witch secured her legs under the roots, bending over at the waist to reach towards the sodden man.

"Grab my arms," she stretched as far as her arms allowed, her cloak falling into his face.

"You can't possibly pull me out," he argued, "the mud is heavy, *I'm* heavy, and I'm stuck—"

"Do as I say!" She roared over the rain.

The Prince heeded her order, wiping his hands as free of mud and water as best he could on his ruined jacket before reaching upwards She clasped him around his forearms, and he did the same, locking together before she pulled him towards her, her stomach burning as she did, with strength far greater than what her body should allow.

He cried out at the stretch, his body moving bit by bit out of the mud, his shoulders screaming. She did not let up, not until one of his legs popped free and he caught hold of the tree with his boot, helping her to pull him out fully.

The earth let him go with a wet pop. He flew up at her faster than expected, propelled by her strength, but her reflexes were sharp. She straightened her back, the roots around her legs groaning, holding his arms while he scrambled for purchase to sit in the roots next to her, his lungs heaving with effort.

He looked like a drowned rat—muddy, miserable, and shivering from the cold. She was not sympathetic.

"You absolute idiot," she shouted at him, gripping his shirt and shaking him despite the ordeal they'd just weathered, "you stupid, foolish boy! Did you not see the rain when you left your city? How did you know I would find you? That you wouldn't be trapped under sheets of mud and rock before I did?"

Rorian grasped her wrists, more to plead she stop the shaking than to pry her away, "I didn't, and you're right, and I'm sorry, but I couldn't...I couldn't be there tonight. They've arrested a man—a good man, a friend—and I found out and I just..."

Slowly the shaking stopped. The witch looked at him with new eyes. At the redness in his, the hoarse edge to his voice.

Had he been crying?

The anger in her vanished. She set him upright, releasing her hold on him.

"I had to get away," he swallowed, not meeting her gaze. "I just...started walking. And then I was walking here, to you and the weather turned and I..."

The witch softened, even in her fear and rage. The changeling scrambled itself up next to them, also panting from how quickly they'd arrived. They were all a state, covered in mud and twigs, drenched in rain and exhausted and frightened. The prince was worse off of all of them.

She turned the way he'd come. "Well you're not going back home," she decided for him, seeing the mess the path had become.

"What now?" He asked, shivering and hugging his arms tightly around himself.

With a sigh she turned to find the path she'd come, not too far off. "We trek back to my shelter," she decided. "And get you out of this rain. If you get stuck," she warned him, "I'm not helping again."

He nodded, swallowing any argument. "Deal."

Chapter Seven

BRAZIERS

"R orian?"

His name was the first word on her lips when she awoke. The fire was fully doused, not even a tendril of smoke rising from the coals. Early morning light, gray with the first dredges of dawn illuminated him from the edge of the alcove, his torso bare to the chill. His scent enveloped her, the warmth of his shirt draped across her like a blanket. The rain had become a light sprinkling, patches of white sunshine breaking the clouds overhead.

"The braziers are lit," he observed, his eyes trained far away on his castle home.

The witch pushed herself up with one arm, pausing to yawn.. "Is that important?"

"It means there's an execution today," his voice somber.

The witch slid to her feet, plodding on silent steps to stand beside him. She grabbed his shirt up on her way to him, turning to see what he saw.

Spots of orange glows dotted the horizon along the western wall of the castle, each a beacon of the death to come. A harbinger of the king's will done.

She held the shirt closer like a safety net. As if it could save her from the grim fate of a stranger so far away.

"Do you need to return?"

Rorian breathed out, his eyes still turned towards home. "It will be expected of me to attend."

"Are you expected at all of them," she inquired, "or just this one?"

His voice was a whisper when he answered, "All of them."

They stood in silence together for a few precious moments more. She leaned against him, for his comfort as much as her own. When his arm came to hold her waist she did not move away.

"They hold them on the wall," he continued, speaking out of a need to open up. She listened. "The wind throws the smoke and ashes onto our eyes, but still we have to watch."

"How does he do it?" She asked.

"It depends on the prisoner." Rorian stepped away, collecting his boots from against the wall and stepping into each one. "My father's always preferred the sword."

"Does he kill them himself?"

"Often," he laced them up, turning his face to her at last. "When the crime warrants it so."

She remembered the day her caravan had been decimated, the large black horse that had led the charge. "That does not surprise me."

"It doesn't?" He asked, tilting his head again. The curiosity no longer irked her, instead she found it endearing. Cute, even. A child with eyes for the world.

Yet Rorian was no child.

"Travel safe," she instructed, handing back his shirt. He slipped the fabric over his head, and she reached out without thought to properly lace and tie the neckline. She wanted to keep her hands busy, to sit with this information and avoid thinking about what he was traveling to see.

Rorian's hand came up to hold hers, his beautifully tanned skin overlaying her indigo in perfect contrast. His eyes found hers, swimming with so many emotions and thoughts. Resolution, an edge of guardedness she'd not yet witnessed upon him, for what he was to face. Mourning. Then a gentleness he reserved only for her.

"I will return when I can," he promised.

"I know." And she would be here, waiting. For that was what time without him had become. Waiting for his return.

Rorian gently lifted her hand to his lips, kissed her palm in farewell. "I'll see you soon, Witch."

She could only nod. Yet being called what she was...she could bear it no more. Not from him.

"Eheren," she spoke the name, sounding it out for the first time in years. "My name was Eheren."

Rorian's breath caught, his eyes widening with surprise. Then his body relaxed into an easy smile.

"I'll see you soon," he breathed, still holding her hand. "Eheren."

She swallowed a tightness in her throat, nodding. Rorian pulled away with reluctance, taking five steps backwards to linger on her, his eyes dancing over her.

And then he turned, and was gone.

And they both faced their days alone.

~ Chapter Eight ~

LEY

It was twilight before Rorian returned. His scent clung to the blankets they'd shared brushing against her senses every time she passed by. Eheren didn't leave the cave much at all that day, instead cleaning and organizing and cleaning again to pass the time.

The changeling was happy to stick around well into the afternoon before catching an errant mouse for lunch that had wandered inside. It finished its meal, left her the bone remains and with a long stretch of its body shifted into a bird and left her in solitude.

She ate. Cleaned herself off with water falling from the trees above. Worried. Paced. Then started the ritual again. Repeatedly. She wore her new cloak that smelled like him, both easing the pain of his absence and compounding it tenfold.

What has gone wrong in my head? She wondered to herself, refusing to admit the truth that was growing in her heart.

Something had changed between them last night. Enough for her to give him her *name*.

She replayed the sound of it on his lips again and again, wishing she could hear it in person. She wanted him to call for her every day, to feel him against her side when he needed comfort or slept through the nights. She couldn't escape images of his body and the scars he wore, nor the way his hair curled when it was wet, his laughter nor voice.

Eheren.

She may be the witch, but he had clearly cast some sort of spell on her through his delicious food and intoxicating aroma.

The fire was just going as night fell when she gave up hope on his return. Not even a heartbeat later she heard the familiar sound of his footfall outside.

Eheren nearly jumped to her feet to meet him at the entrance, finding he had no trouble today climbing up the roots.

Ashes still sat in his hair, the heavy scent of wood smoke and blood smothering his familiar scent. He wore the day so heavily, his shoulders hunched from the effort of it all. She stepped forward, her hand extending towards him. Rorian raised his head to her, his green eyes dulled. They brightened a spark when they met hers, the idea of a smile forced onto his lips.

"I..." He began, but the words choked him. Eheren stepped closer again, and then was standing just before him, his face in her hands.

"Are you alright?" She asked, knowing he wasn't.

He started at the touch, then leaned heavily into it. Let himself crash down from the day and press against her solidness, and began to weep.

Heavy, unbidden sobs tore through him, tears falling faster than she could wipe them away.

"Breathe, Little Prince," she whispered to him, "you're here now."

"He was a squad leader," Rorian choked out, "one of our own. Tried for treason and disobeying a direct order, I...I knew him. Growing up, we...we've clashed swords, broken bread, I watched him court his wife..."

Her heart broke for this human man. For the agony of losing someone you knew, the grief of watching it happen. It was a pain she knew all too well. In that moment he wasn't the man she'd come to know, or the Prince he played back home. He was a boy, raw to the world and burned from it.

She knew what she needed to do. Even if she wasn't sure she should.

"Follow me," she stepped away, gently pulling him along to the entrance of her hollow. "This way, breathe, walk with me..."

Rorian followed her without thought, accepting her words against the blank slate of his mind. Too tired and pained to think on his own.

She took his hand in hers as soon as they landed on the soft ground, refusing to let go their entire trek into the darkness.

The witch led her prince to the lake he'd found her at all those weeks ago. The area they'd set up as a bonfire was tilted in muddy chaos, more work she'd take on another day. The logs were fine enough, though, and she draped her cloak against the one she'd claimed as hers.

"Strip," she ordered him for the second time in two days.

A weak smile graced his lips. "You're making a habit of that request, Eheren."

A thrill went through her when he spoke her name, settling next to her nerves. Her concerns were real that the Ley would once again not answer her call tonight. But this spell was not for her, and she was praying for understanding.

"It's not cold today," she teased him back, "so you can't use it as an excuse this time."

"Why do I need to disrobe?" he asked, crossing his arms over his chest.

"I would think swimming in a lake fully clothed to be uncomfortable, but it's your call."

He tilted his head, curious at what she had in mind, but obeyed. She helped him unlace his boots while he peeled away his ashen shirt and jacket, and left him to remove his pants.

"All of it," she confirmed before he could ask, moving towards the water without waiting. He slid out of his drawers and followed her.

The stars parted in a ripple where they stepped in, flowed away and back to meet their shadows on the water.

Rorian let her lead him along, never letting go of her touch. She held one hand on his shoulder, the other holding his hand, and walked him in until the water came to cover her breasts and half his chest.

"I expected it to be colder," he remarked, meaning the water.

"The sun worked its job after the clouds cleared today," she explained, "thankfully. I've done this in winter before. It was miserable business."

"Done what, exactly?" His head tilted again, and she couldn't help but smile. He was like her own little pup, always following her about.

"A ritual of remembrance," she explained, holding her hands cupped just above the water's surface between them, "to honor those that we've lost."

His silence was solemn as he watched her, the remembrance of his day returning. She released a breath, closed her eyes, and spoke down to the Ley she could feel beneath the lakebed.

Please, she begged of it, *for him, and for the fallen soul you have reclaimed.*

The magic came slowly at first, as if unsure of her true intentions. Only after she began to gather it in her hands, a warm glow sparking there, did it relax and flow more freely. She breathed out again, thanking the Ley with everything she had in her and opened her eyes to him.

His own shone bright with wonder, staring at the raw, glowing flame she held. It was quiet, not quite full, and danced along her skin without a burn.

"Cup my hands," she ordered, and he did, his warmth welcoming after a long day without it. She looked into the glow with him, breathing words from her mind into the spell.

Against the pyres he'd died, in this fire he will be remembered.

"*Speak his name,*" she instructed, her voice sounding so far away, the magic pushing her back and taking control. It had been so long since the Ley had listened to her so clearly, flowed under her stained skin and blossomed through her.

Not since she'd abused it to take lives.

But not even the magic of the earth would deny a soul the right to be honored, even if its conduit was someone as forsaken as her.

Rorian's eyes danced with the light of the flame. "Isaac Harding," he breathed into the flame, and it grew with the offering. Shaped itself round and bright, glowing with importance.

"Speak of Isaac Harding," she guided him, the same way her mother once had when she'd been taught this spell of remembrance, "let the Ley glow with his memory, let him never be forgotten by this world."

Rorian looked away, then back to her again. "Is it right?" He whispered, meek and unsure. "To speak highly of a man executed for crimes against the crown?"

"The Ley burns for no king," she told him, "it listens to no laws but its own. All souls rise from the Ley, and to the Ley they will again fall. Teach the world who he was in your heart. Not who your mortal laws deemed him to be."

Rorian seemed to chew this over, and for long moments she wasn't sure he'd speak again. "He was...a friend," he said at last, his finger pads pressing gently against the backs of her hands, the flame of the Ley between them. "An honorable man, one quick to laugh who stumbled over himself at every opportunity to speak to a girl, until the right one finally came along..."

Once he started, Rorian couldn't stop. Words spilled from him like waterfalls about the man he'd known, tales of hoarding rations to thicken the soup of his men, about how he'd chased after Rorian's older brothers his whole life, closer to them in age than the youngest prince. Each tale painted a picture of who he'd been to Rorian, a surrogate brother, a friend, a partner in small crimes. He spoke of his swordplay, his wife and their child, the way he'd grown from a determined young teen to a leader of men.

The flame grew with his tales, the light inside turning gold, then white, burning brightly for the soul he called to. Isaac Harding. A life that had been, and now a life taken away.

The ending he'd seen himself.

Rorian spoke of that, too. Told the flame of how he held his head high, faced his death with honor and never wavered, never gave in to fear. Of his loss by the sword, of the blood that had spilled.

Of his wife's name on his tongue, the last thing he thought of before the Ley reclaimed him whole.

Eheren listened, but the story wasn't for her. She was only there to channel the flame and be a comforting presence for the prince in his grief. Just as her mother had been to so many during Eheren's young life.

She remembered holding the flame she spoke her mother's name to, and her father's, her uncle's and aunt's and so many more. It had been small but there, alone in the bottom of the world locked away in that cell.

She wondered if anyone would speak her name into the Ley, when she was gone. If the Ley would even listen for what she'd done.

Slowly his words stopped, trickled away into quiet remembrance. Tear streaks had cut through the ashes on his face, until he'd gone on so long they'd begun to dry. He looked exhausted, but by the time he finished a part of his glow that had been missing upon his return was there, hiding in his soft, curious expression.

"We pass Isaac Harding into your light," Eheren breathed to the flame only when she knew he had nothing more to say. She leaned forward, kissing the flame in gentle gratitude for the soul's story it now held, a gesture that made Rorian's eyes go wild with fear that she would be burned.

But the Ley does not burn. It never hurts, only aids the world.

She was the one who had caused it to harm.

The flame danced between them, and then slowly it began to rise. Sections of light pulled away from the glowing orb, falling like gentle flakes of snow down her fingers and to the water below. There it gathered with the stars, floating on the top of the water, dispersing back to the world Issac had once called home.

Rorian watched with rapt interest, his lips slightly parted as he turned this way and that to see the glowing bits float away, then break into smaller motes, then sink into the water like glitter towards the Ley deep below. In minutes her hands lay empty, the last bit of flame slipping between their grasp.

She let out a long breath, releasing the magic she'd held. *Thank you,* she sent her thoughts to the Ley, *for doing this for him.*

She knew it was not for her sake it had answered her call.

"Eheren," Rorian breathed, his hands still holding hers aloft, "I... I have no words."

She smiled. "There's a first for everything."

"No, I mean, yes, but no that's not what I meant." He stepped closer, his eyes searching hers, begging her to understand.

He closed their hands together, pressing them between their chests. "That was... you are amazing. Stellar, even. I've never seen anything like it."

"Thank the Ley," she murmured in response, "it was for you it answered my call,"

"But it was *your* call," he pressed, "*your* magic. It was you, I could feel you in every bit of that spell, tracing into me like a caress. I felt you, Eheren. Not the Ley. Not magic. You. And you are something beautiful to behold."

Pain stabbed deep in her heart. She moved to step away, but his hands tightened on hers.

"Please don't run from me," he begged of her, "you're always so quick to run."

"Don't put me on a pedestal when you cannot understand what I am," she begged in return, "what being a wild witch truly means."

"Then tell me what it means," he shook, "let me in."

"It means I am a monster," she lashed out, "a horrid creature that would take the love and light of the Ley and use it for harm. I've taken lives with that magic, Rorian, even when the Ley screamed in agony as I did it, I did not stop."

"You had your reasons," he said, "it was for your own life that–"

"No one's life is above the will of the Ley," she countered, "I was born entrusted to use it properly, and I took that trust and snarled it like brambles for my own selfish whims." She raised her hands between them, his own refusing to let go. Her indigo skin was black in the low light around them. "That is not the sign of beauty, prince, it is the mark of a monster. I am a monster, don't you see that? Don't you understand what I am now?"

"You *are* beautiful," he did not deny her statement, only added his own. "And I love you as you are. I've never known anything else."

Her lungs caught in her throat, the very forest around them hiding still at his admission

I love you as you are.

Love. He loved her, had fallen through the cracks of the world and into her heart just as surely as she'd done to his.

A single tear slipped from her eye, something shattering in her chest.

She knew already. Had known for a while. But she couldn't avoid the truth anymore.

She loved this man, craved his presence, and mourned his absence, as he was, as he'd always been to her. Broken, strong, drowning in mud or gathering snares, laughing in the sunlight or crying quietly into her back when he thought her asleep.

"You are beautiful," she breathed, "my Little Prince."

She meant more than his face, his voice, his body. His very soul shone like starlight to her, calling through the darkness of her days and guiding her home.

To him.

When he leaned in to kiss her, she met him without hesitation. His lips were soft, warm against her own. Something inside of her cracked, a wall she'd built to keep the harsh world at bay. She let it crumble away, reached up to entwine herself with him, let her hand move and get lost in his honeyed hair like she'd dreamed about for so long.

His hands found her waist, pulled her close until there was no space between them, their bodies alight with the touch.

Rorian kissed her like he meant to drown in her, losing himself in her warmth, her life. When they finally pulled away both were breathless, the world having shifted beneath their feet. It was a welcome change.

The air between them was electric, the moon reflecting in their eyes.

Eheren ran her hands through his hair, pushing it away from his face. "Have you ever been with a woman this way?"

His eyes burned into hers like smoldering coals.

"No," he admitted, "and even if I had...none of them could compare to this moment with you."

The witch smiled.

"Then I will teach you," she breathed, leaning in to whisper the words in his ear, "so many things, if you'll let me."

The prince swallowed, his heart quickening in his chest, "I want to learn everything you have to give, Eheren."

Hearing her name on his lips was an electricity that jolted to her core and threatened to burn her alive from the inside out.

"Rorian," she breathed, because names have power, and she wanted to give this to him, another spark of magic in the night.

They made love in a pool of stars, two souls that had stumbled so alone through this world until they'd found each other. A witch forsaken by the Ley, and the man who loved her in spite of it.

And for everything Eheren taught him, he guided her blind into a new kind of magic, one she'd never hoped to grasp. One that only he could have brought to her.

She burned with it.

Freedom, at last, from her own prison.

~ Chapter Nine ~

HOME

Her days were different, now.

On the nights Eheren slept alone she still found a way to watch the castle from afar. Only now she trained her eyes in the eastern wing's windows, towards his rooms. He'd pointed them out after their night in the lake, drying by the fire in her small cave.

She wondered if a part of her only the Ley could understand had driven her to watch the walls every night, if it wasn't her cell she'd craved but the part of her own soul Rorian had carried with him all this time.

She clutched the shirt he'd left behind to her chest, surrounding herself with his scent, and waited for home to return.

The prince drifted through life in the city, still smiling and laughing with the guards he sparred with, still suffering dinners with guests or his brothers when they returned home.

But every window he passed, his eyes would turn to the woods. Often he was caught lost in the scenery, his eyes distant, his hand covering the place in the center of his chest she now kissed every time he left. The ghost of her touch stayed with him long after he'd lost sight of her, but he ached for the real thing.

The castle no longer felt like home. It had become just a pile of stone and brick, his heart somewhere far away.

It danced over water on the night of the full moons, napped in the trees and taught him more than just magic. Now that she'd grown fond of him, there was plenty of that, too. Magic. Small spells to strengthen tree limbs she climbed, or call the fish of the lakes to her. It was beautiful, watching these little pieces of who she was before his father had torn her down, slowly returning.

When he lay in his own bed he left space for her that he knew she'd never occupy. Dreamed of sharing a pillow and holding her while she slept in his arms.

The bedroom he'd grown up in felt empty, like something was missing. Only nothing had been taken away—he'd just learned what he'd never had.

Such distractions of the heart were not without consequence.

"Are you well?" Jordan leered down at him, tilting his head.

Rorian coughed on the packed dirt, his ass having been handed to him for the third sparring match in a row. His sword was lodged in the ground somewhere out of his reach, and he could feel three new shallow cuts in his bicep for his carelessness.

"Never better," he wheezed to his next eldest brother, picking himself up to a sitting position. "Why do you ask?"

His brother was taller than him, his chest broadened with muscle. They had the same fair hair, and same eyes, but Jordan kept his hair shaved close to the scalp out of function instead of form. It was better than Mikaeus, the oldest, who grew his so long it curled at the nape of his neck and, at times, could be pulled back. Mikaeus had the air of an eligible bachelor, Rorian a socialite, and Jordan, well...he looked like a warrior because he was one.

Jordan waved his hand in a circle in front of Rorian's face. "Because wherever you are, it's not here. If you were to walk out into a serious fight like this you'd be dead within moments."

"Good thing I'm a strategist instead of a warrior like you or Mikaeus," he dismissed his concerns, "us politician-types rarely see a battle more threatening than stroking an advisor's ego with one hand and telling him he's full of shit with the other."

"Be serious," his brother offered his hand; his temple still bandaged from his last journey on military business, a near escape he was clearly projecting onto him. "You may not see battle regularly, but you can't coast through life expecting to survive in a cushy war room."

Rorian took his hand, accepting his aid in uprighting himself. "If you and Mik do your jobs right, that's *exactly* what I plan to do."

"Rory," his brother didn't let go of his hand, tightening the hold. "I'm not always home, but the guards talk to me. They say you've been like this for weeks, getting battered on the training grounds, not paying attention to any real conversation, disappearing off into the woods for two days at a time. What are you even doing out there?"

Living. For the first time in my life.

"I don't have arrows volleyed at me every day like you," he argued defensively, "but the work I do here *is* stressful. I've found time in the woods to be... significantly less so."

"You're trying to tell me you're going camping?" He asked, bewildered, "Communing with trees instead of focusing on your work?"

He thought about a plethora of things Eheren had taught him against trees, and fought the rising blush overtaking his face.

"I'm finding balance in my life," he snapped, pulling his hand back, "maybe that's something you should do as well."

Rorian stormed off the dirt pitch, yanking up his sword along the way.

He was out of sight before his eldest brother stepped out from the shadows, his arms crossed over his leathers and coming to stand by Jordan.

"You think there's a girl?" Jordan asked. Mikaeus snorted.

"Oh there's *definitely* a girl."

~ Chapter Ten ~

LOST

Eheren hovered over Rorian, her hair cascading around him in wild onyx curls, her lips trailing his skin in slow, pleased kisses. There was no rush tonight. Only each other, the low lights of their dying fire, and the afterglow of time spent in her bed once more.

She was wearing his dark tunic, the neckline unlaced where she'd undone it on him an hour before, the hem falling to her mid-thigh. Rorian had one hand on that thigh, the other drawing non-sensical circles on her lower back over the fabric.

He chuckled, letting her nip at his throat. "Was that your way of thanking me for dinner?"

She kissed the spot she had just bit. "It was an excellent dinner."

"I was quite fond of dessert myself," he teased, "if that's my re-ward for lamb legs, I'm afraid the castle chef won't find any left in his store room when next I return."

"I don't think I could eat *that* much."

"I'll make it every night for the rest of our lives," he said, kissing her lips when she moved to sit up. "At least until I find some other meal to top it. Have you ever tried beef steaks? The meat is expensive but absolutely *delicious* in a mushroom sauce."

The smile had slipped from her face at his words. *The rest of our lives.* Slowly she sat upright, looking down on him, the feeling of bliss waning.

He could sense the shift and frowned up at her, worried. "What's wrong?"

"...I shouldn't stay here forever," she spoke into the room, a sentiment she'd ignored every day since she'd settled in these woods and yet...no less untrue. More so now that this new and wonderful thing had entered her life.

The prince's smile was also gone, a seriousness settling over him. "Where would you go?"

She shook her head. "I don't know."

"Back home?" He guessed, "To family?"

"I have no home to return to," she reminded him, "no family left."

"Some...town, then, where you were raised?"

"We were a transient people," she explained, pushing some of her hair behind her ear; it didn't stay there long.

"My house was a wagon, my yard the open roads all across the country. We bathed in pools beneath waterfalls and traded for our fares. We never settled."

"Why not stay here?" He asked, shifting her weight down his hips so he could prop himself up on his elbows. "You're clearly fond of the woods."

A deep ache bloomed in her chest, for herself more than anything. Rorian sensed her silence was more than avoidance of the question, and it was so very like him to guess at the heart of it correctly. He took her chin between his fingers, turning her to face him.

"Hey," he soothed her, "why did you stay here?"

In answer Eheren turned to the opening of her hollow, through the dark roots to the far away lights of the capital city.

"...I spent so many years in that darkness," she told him, "no lights until the guards brought us food, no fresh air or hope to ever breathe it again. The rats, my only friends. Those king's men erased me, killed my family and stole my home. Then they took away chunks of my soul again and again until all I had was that dark, dank space around me. When I escaped and stepped into the night air I breathed it in and expected freedom to taste so sweet."

He watched her speak, gingerly stroking his thumb along her jaw.

"But I didn't know how to live in it." she continued, "Fresh air tasted foreign and unfamiliar. I pushed myself regardless, left the castle walls and ran for the edge of the city. No one stopped me. I made it into the woods and I ran and I ran until my weakened legs finally gave away. I fell into the hollow roots under a tree and hid, terrified that someone would find me and drag me back into the darkness. And yet when no one did..."

She swallowed. Her eyes had begun to mist, the first tears she'd felt since her grand escape,

"At first, I thought it a blessing. Soon enough, I knew it was a curse. All I *was* was trapped in that cell. And once the bars were gone...I had nothing. The part that had pushed me to slay those guards and run as far as I had was the only thing screaming at me to keep running, to go further and further away until that damn castle was a speck on the horizon. The rest of me knew there was nothing to run to. I was no one, I had no name, no magic, and no corner to press my back into when I slept. Only the roots of an unfamiliar tree."

Rorian had gone very still, his eyes wet as he followed her story. His thumb came to wipe the single tear that fell from her eye. She turned to his hand, covered it with her own and kissed his palm.

"I missed it," she finally admitted, mumbling the words against his skin, "I wanted to crawl back to my hole and close the gate and never leave again. The agony of freedom was scalding, it burned within me, and every night I slept where I could see the castle afar in hopes at least visually I could..." her voice caught, shaking as more tears fell.

"If I could see it, remember it was there, so close to me, maybe I could sleep and dream of it. I was too scared to go back, but I've also been too scared to leave. I was trapped in a hell worse than captivity, worse than freedom. And then..."

She looked at him, at the tears running down his own cheeks.

"And then there was you. And now you're here with me, only ever on borrowed time, and I can't go to where you are and you can't come to me and I can't stay here but I would rather tear out my own heart than leave you behind, and I don't even know where I'd go to begin with and you're offering to cook dinner *for the rest of our lives–*"

Her words failed her, deep, broken sobs overtaking her body. Rorian pulled her against him, wrapped his arms around her tightly and rolled until they were safely tucked beneath the blankets, nothing existing but each other, together, safe in each other's arms.

Eheren sobbed into his shoulder. He drew soothing circles on her back, whispered soft platitudes into her hair and held her like he could make everything right if only he didn't let go. He cried silently for her pain, his heart shattering in his chest for what his own father had done to the woman he now loved.

The list was damning. Stole her as a girl, broke her and tortured her until freedom felt like raking hot coals over her skin, killed everyone she'd ever known, and left no home to return to.

This wasn't the image of his father he'd held in his mind growing up, and yet the proof was wrapped around him, holding him tightly and shaking as if to beg him to make it right. To fix her. Only he didn't have the slightest clue where to begin.

He couldn't erase her pain, her past. All he could do was cling to her and weather out this storm and hide in the darkness beside her.

The fire had all but died out when at last she quieted, exhausted. She breathed in his scent with each slow, steady breath, her eyes closed while he left gentle kisses along her head.

"I'm sorry," she rasped, her voice raw from crying.

"Don't ever apologize for needing to feel things," he kissed her forehead again. "I'm here for you."

"I know."

"I love you," he promised her, "as you are."

"So you've said."

"That hasn't changed."

She went limp at that, not realizing how much she'd needed to hear those words. "I'm broken," she whispered.

"Then I'll hold you together."

"Stay," she begged him, "at least for tonight?"

He'd said when he'd arrived in mid-afternoon that he would have to return before darkness fell. It was long past that point, and there was no way he was going to leave her now. Not when she asked him like this.

"I'm here," he agreed, moving to gently disengage from her. "Let me find my pants and stoke the fire, and I'm yours for the night."

Eheren could only nod, feeling surprisingly small. She watched him go about his tasks, turned on her side with her hand lying before her. The indigo skin reminded her of what she'd done, a mark that would never go away.

And yet it was these stained hands he'd let touch him, these stained hands that had even allowed him to enter her life.

Eheren closed her eyes, floating in the lightheaded space after a good cry until he returned to her, tucking them both in and pulling her against his chest. She felt him yawn and settle in.

"Someday," he promised her, "we'll build a new home. Together. Just for us."

She didn't have the strength to argue. It was no small matter that he was a prince who could not walk away from his duties, and she was a scorned witch who would be welcomed by no one, neither her witches nor man. Instead, she let herself believe him, if only while they lay together, and drift off to sleep to the steady rhythm of his heart.

Rorian should have left the night before, he knew, because he was expected back home within the hour for a meal with his family. Nothing so out of the usual when both his brothers came back home, but his absence would not please anyone, he knew.

Still, it was hard enough to pull away from the witch whose bed he'd shared any morning, especially since she was still folded up beneath the blanket he'd gifted her, sleeping in as she always did. After last night he found it nearly impossible to go, wanting to stay and keep her close until they could work out this mess of impossibility before them.

More importantly, he couldn't find all his clothes.

"Love?" He asked, looking around the blankets, "Where is my shirt?"

"Hmm?" She kept her eyes closed, sleep heavy in her voice. "I don't recall you wearing one."

He looked at the slip of dark fabric peeking out from under her hair like a pillow. "...I'm not getting that back any time soon, am I?" He couldn't help but smile.

"I'll bite if you try." Eheren curled up around the tunic, nuzzling into the fabric.

"You did warn me that you'd devour me someday."

"I recall something of the sort."

Watching her lay there so peacefully, her tears dried, a light smile gracing her lips, he couldn't bear to tear it from her. With a sigh he slipped his jacket over his bare skin, moving next to lace his boots. "I've got a breakfast to attend," he told her, sitting near her while he worked, "but I'll see if I can't slip away again soon after."

"Your brothers are home?" She guessed, familiar with his daily patterns by now.

"Should have gotten back last night," he confirmed, turning to pet her hair back from her face. One beautiful violet eye cracked open to peek up at him before closing again, too tired to remain open.

"I would stay if I could," he promised her.

"Just now, or forever?"

In answer he leaned in to plant a soft, slow kiss on her lips. "Forever," he breathed, but she was already back asleep. His heart ached to go, her revelations from the night before still heavy on his mind.

They followed him the whole way home, rolling in his thoughts again and again on an endless loop. What he was going to do with them yet, he wasn't sure.

The southern wall of the castle housed the main entrance, so it was easiest to slip back into the city on that side and walk the streets home. He didn't make it past the morning market just beyond the castle wall before he found an apple tossed at his head, barely catching it in time he was so lost in thought.

"There you are," a familiar voice intoned.

Jordan walked towards him with a purpose, looking like he'd barely gotten any sleep the night before. How late had he arrived back in the city?

"I was ten minutes from rallying up a search party to comb the woods."

Rorian sighed, handing him back the apple.

"I would have killed you if you'd done such a thing," he quipped, moving towards the edge of the market. "You're no better than a mother hen herding me about sometimes."

"Then herd yourself to get home at a decent hour," Jordan stepped in front of him, "because instead of being halfway through my breakfast, I'm out here looking for you."

Rorian rolled his eyes. "And you found me, didn't you?"

"You are seriously half out of your mind, you know that?" Jordan took a bite of his apple, made a face, and let it drop to the ground. "Ugh, that's tart. Anyway, you spend half your week daydreaming and staring at trees and the other half doing gods-know-what off in the forest like a vagabond. Father said you were gone most of yesterday, and you didn't even make it back home by the time I rolled in."

"Which was... when, exactly?"

"Don't ask, I'm running on half a night's sleep."

Jordan paused his words, tilting his head to study his brother. "Where is your shirt?" He inquired.

Rorian looked down to his bare chest beneath his jacket. "Oh, uh, it got stuck on some brambles earlier," he lied, "it was easier to slip it off than try and untangle it."

Jordan narrowed his eyes. "Where do you even *sleep* when you're out there?"

"I have a cave that I like. It's quite cozy."

"You never take a horse?"

"It's not that far, I like to make sure I have enough time to travel home within a two-hour walk."

"A horse would be quicker."

A horse might spook at the sight of Eheren. They are not fond of wild witches.

He dismissed his brother's concern with a wave of his hand. "If you're so worried about my free time you're welcome to join me," he gambled.

Jordan's face screwed up in displeasure. "I have enough roughing it on the roads for my job, why in the hell would I want to suffer the outdoors at my leisure?"

Rorian shrugged, stepping past him. "I guess that's just another perk of being a spoiled courtier; I find nature to be quite lovely."

His brother caught up to him in two long strides, falling into step by habit. "Oh, what a horrible life you lead."

"I prefer it to being a grunt soldier."

"Hey," Jordan snapped, "that's *commander* grunt soldier to you!"

"I will never call you anything of the sort," Rorian snorted, "as I do not respect you."

"Clearly," he said, walking them through the castle gates and towards the side doors that would take them quickly to the dining hall, "a free piece of information? Father is not pleased by your tardiness."

Rorian groaned. "A price I was expecting to pay, but am not looking forward to."

Jordan slapped his back hard enough to make him wince. "Don't worry, baby brother," he said, laughing. "I've got your back. And it's only one meal, how bad could it go?"

Rorian's mind was still far away, ruminating on the pain of his lover and the horrors she'd faced. "Can't be that bad," he agreed, following his brother towards their castle.

~ Chapter Eleven ~

CAPTURE

It was a rare treat to have all four of the Delafoy men under one roof anymore. While Rorian stayed close to the castle going ons, only taking brief breaks to travel as far as Eheren's waiting arms, his brothers were constantly out in the world, and his father busy with running a kingdom.

Jordan spent long stints rallying arms against the proposed danger the witches posed, and Mikaeus worked far more dangerous missions. Information was his game, and for it, he was good. Nearly the right hand to the king and the crown prince set to take the throne one day, he took on errands not even Rorian was privy to, and it kept him away for sporadic stretches of time.

Today they sat at a long rectangular table, King Fallon at its head, still dressed in ceremonial attire from the morning's church-going events. Jordan sat to his left in dark military clothes,

Makaeus to his right in a relaxed tunic and pants, a gold crown on his head in a half-hearted attempt to look his station. Rorian hadn't even bothered, smelling of dirt and moss, his woods-stained cloak draped across the high back of his chair. He'd fastened his jacket shut to hide his lack of a shirt, something Jordan had silently judged him for.

They looked like actors in a particularly chaotic play. It was Rorian's luck his father did not demand formal outfits for these meals, as he didn't want to waste more time changing and prolong his ire. He'd been late enough.

Mikaeus and their father were already on their second course when Jordan and Rorian arrived, not having bothered to wait. Their plates were sitting out already, a bowl of soup at each place with breads and cheese to start.

"You're late," King Fallon Delafoy pointed out, raising an eyebrow to his youngest's arrival.

His crown sat beside him on the table, a heavy silver piece the church had crafted themselves with large sapphire stones and carvings of their gods.

"Forgive me," Rorian had asked of him, taking his usual place at the opposite end of the table, "I lost track of time last night and ended up camping in the woods rather than walking back in the dark."

"What is it you do out there, exactly?" Mikaeus asked, a bemused smile on his face. "Father thinks you're taking after our mother, getting lost in nature, but I've got a theory you've come to enjoy mushrooms perhaps a little too well."

"Sorry to disappoint," he picked up his spoon, digging into his room temperature soup without complaint, "but I was out fishing."

"How did that go?" Fallon propped his head on his fist in amusement.

"Terribly," he laughed, "I now am without possession of a net nor a single fish."

The lie came to him easily enough. It was true that he didn't have a net or fish, but more because he'd never owned either. Eheren preferred red meats, and he'd only learned to fish as a child. It had been a miserable game of waiting for little reward.

"I thought you said you went on these little wood treks to relax," Jordan shared a look with Mikaeus that Rorian couldn't decipher before continuing, "that hardly sounds relaxing to me."

He sighed. "Most trips go better. I wanted to try something new."

"That was your mistake," Mikaeus shrugged, and just like that, the inquisition on his journey came to an end. For that he was grateful.

The brothers talked to their father while they ate, telling him of their latest journeys, answering any questions he had about the movement of men or rumors that had reached his ears. It was all their usual business banter. Rorian ate in silence. He found himself studying his father and feeling a million miles away from the three men he loved so dearly in his heart.

Fallon was tall and lean, as they all were. Their signature honey hair had come from him, drowning out their mother's fiery red locks and freckled complexion. Their marriage had been a political one, but a rare gem rooted in love. Mikaeus called it an *obsession*. When she'd been alive, Fallon had been a force of a man, stood as tall as any tree, shone as bright as the sun. He'd been broader then, still active in the military pursuits that'd earned his fame just as sure as any decisions from the throne.

Now, he'd slimmed from age and her loss, streaks of white and grey growing at his temples and in his short-trimmed beard. His sharp green eyes were shadowed with dark circles beneath, and lines creased their edges. Even with time and grief doing their work he sat with a straight back, his shoulders strengthened from his place in the world.

He looked like a king. He looked like their father.

But did Rorian really know him?

Fallon Delafoy was royalty to the bone. The eldest of three brothers he'd been raised into duty, molded and formed into a ruler by the stern hand of Rorian's late grandfather. Rorian had grown up with stories of how, by the tender age of five, his father could recite the name of every country, city, and ruler on the entire continent, and knew all their major imports and exports by six.

Rorian had only been a year behind, memorizing dry texts and trade ledgers by seven. As the youngest son, there was never any expectation that he would rule, but he'd strived to find his place in this court as his father had. Where his brothers picked up swords and forged their names in blood and glory, Rory had learned the intricate dance of socialites. His brothers could split a man's throat by ten. Rorian could navigate a cut-throat room of dignitaries, advisors, and— worst of all—their wives by the same age.

Eheren had told him once that words were their own kind of magic, and it was a spellwork he was very familiar with. His father had recognized his talents, praising him for his quick wit and intelligence all his life, and granting him more space at the table for it as he grew.

Today, though, Rorian did not seek his praise. He was withdrawn into himself, warring with the patient, unflappable ruler he knew his father to be, and the cruelties he now knew he'd committed. Fallon had not faulted Rorian for crying after his mother's death, instead closing his office door, embracing his son and crying with him, teaching him that even the best ruler is human. That more than a king, he could be a father when his son needed him most.

"It will be alright," he'd promised him, caressing the back of his teenage son's head like he was a child, "I will make it so."

Seemingly, he had. In the six years since, he'd risen to meet the tide of resistance the witches put up against his throne, all started by one lone agent who took the life of his late queen. He'd secured weapons and spoke at soldiers' funerals about their sacrifice and valor against such a formidable enemy. "We will not bow," he was oft to say, "we will not bend beneath their pressure."

All the while, Rorian had worked his own skills. He'd secured trade deals for steel, smoothed out the concerns of lords *furious* their sons were called to battle, and put on the brave face of a son who knew his father was hurting as much as he and taking on any task asked of him.

That was his guilt to bear. He'd eaten dinners and shaken hands while Eheren and so many others rotted away in his own basement. He'd unwittingly helped spread lies and ignorance of the witches and propagated this genocide in part. His brothers may have blood on their swords, but his hands were far from clean in this.

The same hands that held his lover had signed deals in his father's name that aided in the slaughter of her people.

And he hated himself for it. It made him sick.

Rorian ground the heels of his palms into his eyes, trying to focus back in on the table around him before he was called out for his absence.

"Your information was correct," Mikaeus told their father, setting his spoon on his bowl. "I just heard back from the men I sent."

Fallon leaned back in his seat, steepling his fingers. Concern drew lines across his face, showing the king's age.

"They really are sending them to Arohan," he breathed, "Gods above."

"Sending who?" Rorian asked, a small twinge of concern prickling his spine. "Is this about Arohan's recent scuffle with Folvac?"

"No," Mikaeus shook his head, his curling blonde locks moving around the short gold crown he wore. "We received word that there is a movement of witches fleeing to Arohan."

Rorian had a moment to feel his stomach unfurl in relief. Arohan was far from an enemy to their country, but they'd not been allies in a long time. It was the safest option to flee to—a small mountainous country their own could not risk war against without giving up their already restricted trade on raw ores Arohan mined. The witches could be safe there, he figured. Free from the nightmares they awoke to at home.

"Fleeing would be preferable," their father cut his relief short, "they are not sending the feeble, this is a planned move against us. Once in Arohan they will train the children and send them back ten years forth, a strengthened unit against us."

Children.

"So your informant has told us," Mikaeus agreed. "They leave under a banner of *refugees* that Arohan either truly believes, or has decided to publicly stick by. This could also be their first move against us in a larger conflict."

Children.

"We cannot allow it," Fallon hit his hand on the table, not hard enough to make his plate jump, but enough to emphasize his sincerity.

"Going onto Arohan soil is grounds for a war," Jordan reminded them, "our fight against the witches has been strained enough, if we provoke The Aros into an outright battle, things could go very poorly for us."

"A fact I am well aware of," Fallon leaned forward, picking up his silverware with consideration. "So I don't plan to allow them to cross our borders alive."

Rorian's throat constricted. He cleared it, inadvertently gaining the attention of all three men. "These...refugees," he chose that word, "who are they?"

"Any witch under fourteen from the northern territories," Mikaeus recited from his informant. "Father's eyes have confirmed their purpose; I only confirmed their movement. It's happening, and it's happening soon."

"How soon?" Jordan asked.

"Before summer," Mikaeus told them, "when the rivers through the pass aren't as volatile, but before the heat."

"Then we will act quickly," Fallon decided, "Jordan, I expect your men to be ready within the week. Ride out on horseback and take out their numbers before they leave our borders."

Rorian gaped at them in horror, waiting for someone, *anyone*, to wake up and realize what exactly it was they were proposing. To laugh at the dark absurdity and go back to the talks of training or upcoming summer festivals. None did.

"Yes, your majesty," Jordan affirmed, his voice that of any commanding officer receiving his orders.

"See it done."

The ringing in Rorian's ears threatened to deafen him. He brought to mind an image of Eheren she'd painted for him—small, wild and free, traveling the country with her family, the sun in her air, the wind on her face. Then another, of dark cells and blood and steel.

"You can't," he croaked out, clearing his throat again.

"What did you say?" Mikaeus genuinely didn't hear him.

Rorian exhaled his breath, gripping the edge of the table to steady himself. "I said you can't commit such an atrocity," he let his voice ring clear, strong and sure. "This is not an act of war, this is the slaughter of kids!"

"They are not *kids*," his father spoke evenly, "they are *witches*, tomorrow's soldiers who will come back to finish what their parents could not achieve. Trained magical specialists out for our blood, every last one. You would permit such a force to rally and rise against us? Be reasonable, Rory."

"They are *children!*"

"Have you heard nothing I've said?" Fallon's patience waned.

"Killing children is a monster's errand," he countered, rising to his feet, steadying himself on the tabletop with his palms.

"For the safety of our people, it may be monsters we become," Fallon's voice grew hard, as if speaking to a child. "We have a duty as the royal family to our countrymen, and I will not spare lives today to have more slain tomorrow."

"The only duty you abide by is your own," Rorian finally snapped, raising his voice in anger. It was the first time he had spoken to his father in such a way. "You are sending my brother to *murder* babes on a crusade built on lies—are we not your countrymen too? Do you not have a duty to us, your sons, for the truth?"

"Rorian," Mikaeus stood from his seat, "you are out of order to speak to Father this way!"

"I speak to him today because I know about his experiments in the sub-cellar of the West Wing," Rorian shouted back, refusing to heed his brother's words.

Eheren's pain that he carried twisted like brambles inside of his chest, pushing him on and fueling his fire. He turned back to his father, wielding that agony like a sword.

"I know what you did to all those witches, how you slaughtered families and took captives to experiment on, how you starved them and fed them steel and used them as test subjects for torture methods, weapons, and worse. How you kept them in darkness and pain in your cruelties, unable to even stand upright in their cells. I know how this crusade of yours was built. It was founded on lies against their people and paid for with the blood of those incapable of fighting back!"

"Witches are *monsters*," Mikaeus argued for his father. "Quiet killers who work in the shadows to take the lives of men as they deem fit."

"Witches cannot *use* magic to kill!" he shouted down the table, "They are not magical beings, they are beings of magic! Their power is borrowed and it has rules, but our ignorance of those boundaries has been twisted and used against us for your—" he pointed at his father, "—horrifying *genocidal* use! You've been killing innocents, sending my *brothers* to kill innocents, and for what? Why?"

"A witch killed our mother," Mikaeus nearly laughed, bitter and enraged, "unless you've forgotten!"

"That witch killed no one with magic," he defended, "because any witch who uses magic to harm another wears that transgression stained on their skin, and his hands were clear when he died. I saw the execution myself. You were all there, too. This story doesn't add up. You *lied*," he accused his father, turning back to him and ignoring his brother completely. "And now your lie will cause slews of children, *children* to die screaming deaths. I do not stand for this!"

He threw his goblet across the table, his drink splattering the surface until it rolled off the edge and clattered to the floor. The room was silent, echoing with his words. He did not see the looks on his brothers' faces, because his eyes were only for his father.

For their king.

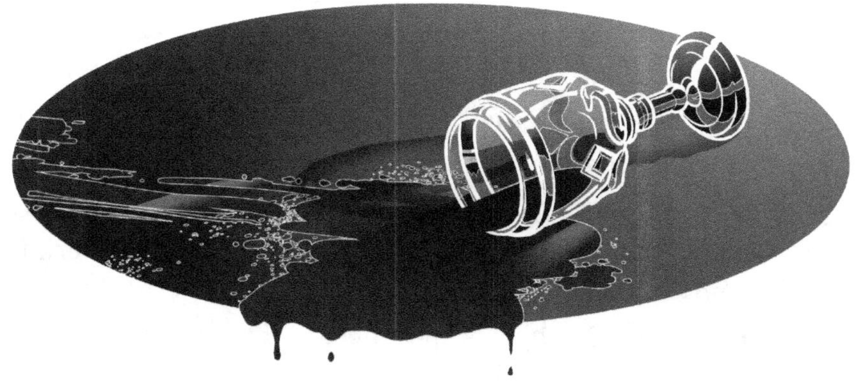

Fallon had not reacted to his son's outburst, nor the accusations slung against him. His eyes had widened for a brief point in time in the beginning, then slowly he'd settled into a long, hard stare at his youngest boy.

Rorian's eyes were fire, anger and rage causing his hands to shake. Until his father broke his silence.

"And how," King Fallon asked in a suspicious tone, "did you come to believe such a story?"

The tremors in his hands stopped. Rorian knew his mistake the moment his father's words were out of his mouth, knew that he'd seen right through him, past the truth laid bare and into the heart of the matter.

Rorian had to have gotten his information from *somewhere*.

From some*one*.

And there was only one person who could have given it to him; a prisoner of those very cells he'd hidden from them all, the only one to escape.

Eheren.

Rorian pressed his jaw together so tight it would be impossible for anyone to tear the words from him. *No,* he thought to himself, *I will not give her up. Not even if I am tortured, not even if they break every bone in my body and tear out my eyes.*

"Do you deny it, then?" Rorian asked instead, refusing to look away from the man, to give him the satisfaction of watching him squirm.

The king stood from his chair, Jordan already out of his as well, too uncertain of what was happening to remain seated.

"It seems the youngest prince has been bewitched," his father spoke to the room, "his mind filled with filth by a dangerous criminal I've known about for months now."

Mikaeus looked as if he'd been slapped. "That's impossible," he rose to step around the table towards their father, "He has not been in contact with the girl—"

"—Who infiltrated the castle and murdered twelve of my best men in cold blood?" His father finished for him. "Oh, I think he has. Where else would such corruption have found its way into his mind?"

"A witch infiltrated the castle?" Jordan sounded so genuinely surprised. "When did this happen? Why was I not informed?"

"...You were away," Mikaeus spoke slowly, as if checking on each word below letting it go. "Father decided you were best kept from the horrors we found."

"When did you become our father's mouth?" Rorian challenged his eldest brother, "Have you finally come so far in your kiss assery you've crawled up and out the other side?"

"Do not hide behind vulgarities," the king said, "our conversation is not finished."

"What conversation?" Rorian turned back to him. "You have yet to deny a word I've said, only hidden behind your son and continued to twist words to your advantage!"

"She's gotten her talons in deep," Fallon said with a note of sadness, as if he felt pity for his poor bewitched son.

His eyes told a different story.

They were hard, colder than he'd ever seen.

If Rorian had ever doubted Eheren of his father's capability, he did no longer.

Those eyes were not the man who raised him. Not the man who cried with him in his study, or praised him for his work, or looked upon his boys as they learned the sword.

The shield of *father* had been wiped clean.

He saw for the first time in his life Fallon Delafoy, the man behind the crown, the man who had hidden behind family and leadership like a snake in the shadows.

And now his fangs were sunk deep into Rorian's heart.

"Guards!" Fallon boomed, and in an instant the doors were open, three men falling in line. "Your youngest prince has been bewitched," he spoke as if from a broken heart.

"What are you doing?" Rorian demanded, stepping back from the table.

"Escort him to his rooms under guard," Fallon continued his decree, "in irons."

"This is too far!" Jordan stood up for his youngest brother, "this must be a mistake, something that can be worked through, a bewitching is not permanent–"

"In the beginning," Mikaeus spoke clear and slow. "A bewitching can be broken in the early stages. If her magic is too far into his mind..."

"It might not be," Jordan tried, but the guards could not ignore the King's orders long.

Rorian made to run, bolting around the range, only to meet the arms of his eldest brother, holding him in place for the guards to catch up. He struggled, shouted, cursed Mikaeus with every breath.

"You align yourself with a deceiver!" Rorian begged his brothers to understand, "he's using you, *both* of you!"

"Be silent," Mikaeus hissed at him. "You are doing yourself no favors."

"You are meant to be King one day," he spat back, "the gods will not forget your hand in this, nor if you kill those children."

Cold iron cuffs came down in his wrists, binding them behind him. He shoved his shoulder into his elder brother to push away, Mikaeus's angelic face unreadable. Rorian did not fight the guards dragging him halfway across the room to the door, walking on his own with their hands around his biceps.

"The witch cannot be far," his father turned to his two remaining sons, stopping Rorian in his tracks. "Jordan, search the woods and have her found. Do not let her live to see the next dawn."

"No," Rorian breathed, then louder, kicking and fighting the guards with all his might. He might as well have been a kitten to a lion for all the good it did him. They picked his feet off the floor, shouting for him to stop. "No!"

"We'll start with the North," Jordan promised, "it's where I saw him returning this morning."

Rorian blinked. It hadn't been the northern wall he'd returned to at all, but the southern. The way he'd always came. And it wasn't like Jordan to make such a careless mistake.

Jordan met his eyes, his jaw tight, and he knew it was not Jordan the King's Second Commander who looked upon him, but Jordan, Rorian's elder brother.

It was all he could do for him in this room.

Thank you, he said with his eyes. Jordan gave no sign that he understood. Then he returned to his struggle, shouting obscenities at the men who handled him.

"Then see it done," Fallon ordered, then turned to his eldest son. "Mikaeus, hold a tribunal for him tonight, determine how deep this spell holds him. If he fails, bring him for trial tomorrow morning. He has much to answer for."

"On what charges?" Asked the crown prince, his face grim but belaying no other hint of his thoughts on the matter.

"For bringing lies into my court and consorting with a dangerous witch?" the King asked, turning to look Rorian in the eyes in the moment before he was pulled into the hall.

"High treason."

~ Chapter Twelve ~

ABLAZE

The witch had settled back into the emptiness of her lover's absence, but this time it felt heavier. He had left her with much to think on.

A future. Eheren hadn't dreamed of such a thing since she was a child, bright eyed and innocent of the horrors she later faced. Her earliest daydreams involved, with no small amount of irony, a prince come to sweep her away to live in a castle. More realistic desires had formed as she grew, such as wanting a wagon of her own and a husband to start a family, while walking the path of spirit aid as her mother had, helping people speak for the dead.

She'd learned plenty of crafts in her life, from weaving to pottery, but she'd never been fond of any art other than magic. She'd cast motes of light with raw Ley above her head on sleepless nights, shaping them into her desires. A faceless husband, a home, her family.

In the cells she'd tried to do the same, but the magic wouldn't come to her around the steel. That cell had robbed her of more than her dignity, her voice, or even her magic. It took away her ability to dream. To think to the future.

All day it tormented her relentlessly, pounding on the doors of her mind as if to demand an audience. *What will you do?* The question threw itself around with reckless abandon, *Where will you go?*

Rorian did not return that night as they'd hoped. The small bed of furs she lay in had never felt so large. His scent clung to her, a ghost against her skin. Sometime in the night she pulled on the tunic she'd stolen from him that morning. It was large on her, the hem brushing her mid thighs like a dress, the sleeves covering her thumbs.

She hugged herself, closing her eyes and imagining it was him. She would need to leave this place, she knew, but the pain kept her here.

It wasn't the call of her cell that burned in her chest anymore. Now it was this stabbing agony at the thought of leaving him.

She couldn't stay.

She couldn't go.

She was lost, broken in new, endless ways.

Sleep came fitfully leaving her to wake far too early. It soured her mood.

Where is Rorian?

She slipped from her cave in the grey light of late dawn, tending to her needs and washing her face in a nearby stream.

When would he return?

Each minute without him was agony, tearing at her soul with claws.

Blearily, she opened the door all those demanding questions had beaten against the day before, and calmly they stepped to greet her.

What now? She asked herself.

Perhaps...when he returned...they could talk. *Would* talk, about...*them*. And their future. About possibilities she'd only just begun to sketch out in her mind.

They could leave together, forget this war and King and land and carve out a new life...somewhere. Where? She didn't know, but Rorian might have an idea on that. He knew so much about this world and all its strange places. She'd listened for endless hours before as he'd talked about countries she'd never even heard of, some only a few days' travel to the next border, others weeks by sea to new lands. She'd seen the ocean before as a child, but she'd never traveled far on one. Perhaps that's where they would find themselves, far across the sea, where no one knew his name or understood what the strange indigo stains on her arms could mean.

If there was no place for them here, then they'd carve out one somewhere else. Together.

She returned to her cave, pacing while she wondered on how to best bring this idea up. She'd been there for barely a few minutes, her newest cloak across her shoulders, his tunic still worn over her body, when the familiar beat of white wings came swooping into her space once more.

The changeling crashed directly into her chest at top speed. It was all she could do to catch him, knocked back by the force.

"Little one," she wheezed, picking herself off the ground while the white bird of the little beastie shook its head and regained his bearing. "You do not need to careen into me, you know I'll share."

She had breakfast going on a small fire behind her, the usual call for the changeling to visit. His visits had become more frequent just as Rorian's had, usually on the days she was without her prince. It helped ease her loneliness, and the only cost was a few bites of any meal.

The bird shook its head, jumping away from her to shift into its favored fox form. He ran in circles around her feet, chittering and jumping towards the entrance.

What now? She wondered, coming to stand beside it. Far off in the grey skies where rain threatened to visit, the castle sat quiet atop the city, a dark smudge on a bleary day.

Then she saw it. The first orange glow of a brazier lit. Then a second, and third, going down in a line. Her heart sank with sympathy for Rorian, knowing another traitor would be executed on the walls, and he would be forced to watch once more.

We can visit the lake again, she was already planning, the fox nipping at her ankles, *if he so chooses.* Since she'd performed the remembrance ceremony the Ley had come easier to her call, cautiously warming up to her once more. It was a welcome old friend, and it felt like a part of her she didn't know was missing had returned with it. A piece of who she was as a witch.

"Ow!" She cried sharply, the fox having sunk its teeth into her lower calf, "what has gotten into you?"

The changeling yelped, barking a strange cry and jumping in place. She'd only begun to examine the bleeding wound when it happened.

The Ley came to her, unbidden, its golden touch snaking through her bones and wrapping around her ears to whisper its call.

Rorian Delafoy, it called, the name repeated in a thousand voices, each climbing over the other to be heard, *Rorian Delafoy!*

No, her heart beat a war drum in her ears, fear swelling within her to push out the Ley calling him back to it, *no!*

The changeling cried as a bird, extending its long white wings and howling back at the Ley, defying its roar. She understood now, hells below, did she understand.

Eheren did not think. She left her fire lit, her meal untouched, and took off towards the city beyond. The changeling flew beside her as she carried forward, hand over hand at times, climbing over roots or racing on long, silent strides. She pushed herself faster than she'd ever gone, all the while the Ley chased at her ankles, grabbing for her, clamoring towards the execution like an unseen wave.

Rorian Delafoy, his name throbbed through the earth, shook the trees and threatened to blind her with the force of its cry.

Rorian, she called out herself, pulling the Ley into her, pushing her legs faster than they were meant to go, feeling the forest around her and mapping her path without sight. Everything was a blur, instinct and fear guiding her towards him.

Towards home.

The city was still asleep, the streets empty at such an early hour. A few people milled about, setting about their day, but none could even see let alone comprehend the wraith that ran around them on silent feet, a midnight cape snapping in her wake. The changeling soared overhead, crying for her to occasionally change directions, helping her navigate the streets for the fastest path.

Before her the castle arose, impossibly tall stone walls surrounding its layered interior. The changeling cried again and she followed, not stupid enough to go in the front door. Alarms would raise and she'd face an army of guards and king's men before she could ever reach the eastern wall, the tallest side facing the far off mountains, that she knew.

The bird led her to the west, to a lower section surrounded by old, tall trees. It was far too high for a mere man to scale, but she was no man.

Eheren climbed a tree the changeling landed on, high enough to lock eyes with the older, less maintained part of the wall about halfway up. The displaced stones could give her plenty of handholds.

Please, she begged of the Ley, borrowing its power once more to pull into her muscles, strengthening her again. Then, with arms outstretched, she leapt.

The stone wall greeted her with a shock of pain, but she held on. With only a second to gather her wit she climbed, the changeling circling behind her, crying for her to hurry, to go faster, to make it.

She reached the top covered in sweat, her heart racing so fast it threatened to beat out of her chest. Her legs and arms shook from the effort, the Ley rolling within her notwithstanding. She wasted no time, knowing the platform on the western wall was only accessible from the ground. It's how she had left the first time, through a large gate and up into the interior stairways wide enough to fit a carriage up. Then she'd thrown herself off the opposite side, falling into a river far below.

With a few breaths and a cry of encouragement from the changeling above her, she took three long, racing steps and threw herself over the inner wall, wrapping the Ley around her like a shield.

She'd landed hard just outside the stables, the smell of hay and horses nearly choking her. Eheren kept her mouth closed against the assault, looking for a way forward. The changeling had not come with her. A magical being had no place in these walls. She was on her own.

Her eyes snapped to the far western wall a distance away, then to the glowing fires atop it. She'd never make it in time. She might already be too late, but even running as fast as she could, even if she did not encounter further resistance this early in the morning... it would take so long to get there. Too long.

She'd barely made it a step before a shadow befell her, eclipsing her in its entirety. Her instincts screamed of danger and she whirled, jumping back from the source.

Heartless, the war horse of King Fallon and legend, lowered his head to her, his eyes black pools. The stories had not done him justice; he was impossibly tall, well into the 18 hands she'd always heard and as wide as four of her. His back was above her head, his jet black coat broken in only a few places by long healed scars. He was a creature of muscle and iron, his lips pulling back to expose large square teeth.

She'd landed directly into his home, a witch laid before him like a meal from the gods.

Her heart quickened, her breath seizing in her throat. She tried to swallow the fear and work through her thoughts, to hear them over the screaming of the Ley.

Rorian, Rorian, Rorian! It howled, impossibly loud for the prince's soul to return home into its embrace.

Not if I have a say in it, she hardened her heart to the fear, locking it away. Be it a man or beast before her, she *would* go through, she *would* reach him in time.

And if she didn't...she would stain every inch of her skin indigo with her sins and red with the blood of this court.

Heartless's ears flicked, his head shaking in irritation. A screeching whinny rose from within him, as if he could hear the Ley's howling and tried desperately to knock it away.

An idea formed in her mind. A dangerous, stupid idea that risked precious time she didn't have.

"You hear it too," she spoke to the horse, his head snapping up in rage that a witch would approach him. He rose himself up to his full, terrifying height. Massive hooves stomped on the ground, the very same that had crushed people to death beneath them.

"You know his name," she continued, taking a cautious step closer. He snorted, braying with his ears back at this approaching creature. "I won't allow the Ley to take him today," she swore to the stallion, cutting open her palm with her long black nails. Blood welled and fell between them, an offering. A bargain.

His nostrils flared, his obsidian eyes boring into hers.

"Please," she begged Heartless, one monster to another, "have a heart."

She held up both of her hands, the scent of her prince still strong on her clothes. She hoped it was enough. She stepped into his range, and he struck out.

When the horse's teeth clamped down on her shoulder, she sank in her own fangs.

~ Chapter Thirteen ~

KINGS

R orian would die within the hour, of this he was certain. He'd made as much peace as he could with it. No one was ever truly ready to die, he learned, even when it was the right thing to do. Even if it saved the woman they loved, and perhaps could change the world.

Or so he'd hoped. He wouldn't very well be around to see the fruits of his labor, if his words would reach the ears of people who mattered. Perhaps he was only fated to become a blood smear on the stones, forgotten by history as the tragic prince who became spellbound and died for his transgressions.

At least this gave Eheren a chance.

The top of the western wall was wider than any other section. It could easily host twenty men side by side, built back when this fledgling kingdom had not been so grand, and the mountains near in the distance were home to another kingdom with blood to claim. The space was designed to hold trebuchets and oil vats against intruders, but that war had been settled long ago and the territory far over the mountains now claimed as their own.

With no real purpose left to it, his great-grandfather had instead used the space for executions in a time of terror within their city. The great metal braziers, when lit, were meant to inspire fear of the crown's might against those who would do them wrong, a tradition carried on by his father today.

He'd been on this platform so many times before. Watched traitors against the crown find their end. His mother had never been fond of the princes witnessing such *horrid things*, in her words, but their father had never been one to coddle them against the harsher parts of being royalty. *People always coveted power*, he'd said, and they were doing the boys no favors by pretending this was not a part of their lives.

Today it would be the final part of his.

No two men were ever the same facing their demise. Some cried and pleaded, begging the gods or their king for clemency. Others bartered, promising gold or favors to anyone who would aid them. He'd seen more than one man wet themselves in fear.

Rorian had had hours to decide how he would die. What kind of man he'd be. And he decided he would die a prince, his head held high until the Ley came to retake his soul.

He wondered if Eheren would speak of him to the Ley when she found out. *If* she'd even find out. When.

Rorian spat blood onto the ground when the last brazier was lit, his tooth reopening a wound in his cheek. Mikaeus had...inquired things of him for hours the night before, and he hadn't been light-handed.

They hadn't found Eheren. When Mikaeus entered his room by late evening, frustration written into his beautiful face, he'd been sure of it. Jordan had led his men on a fool's chase north of the city, illuminating every cave they could find based on what little pieces of truth he'd pieced together from his stories about trekking the woods.

Stay safe, he'd prayed to her, not bothering to ask his gods that had so long ignored the light of the witches, *live another day.*

His relief had been short lived. Mikaeus pulled a chair out for him, the two men he brought along pushing Rorian into the seat. He'd recognized them as his brother's employees by the deep blue clothing they wore, trained specialists who had a way of getting information out of anyone.

His stomach had burned, knowing what they were there for.

"Please, Rorian," Mikaeus had remained standing, his face a picture of worry and concern. "Let me help you."

"You've done enough to help," he'd laughed, "we all have, Mik. I'm surprised you haven't put this together yourself."

"A witch has gotten into your mind," his brother spoke evenly, as if he truly believed it and was trying his best to aid him in this plight. As if all he needed to do was see the light. "A bewitchment has taken hold, it's not too late—"

"For you to see reason," he cut him off, "the proof is in the far western wing, look for a stone door that leads to the sub-basement and the cells within. Go down there yourself and see that—"

"I *went* down there myself," Mikaeus cut him off, and hope rose again in Rorian's chest, only for it to be slashed short with his next words. "There *was* no sub-basement. Not even an entrance."

"How long after I confronted Father did you go?" He accused him, and at Mikaeus's silence he leaned forward, stopped short by two hard hands on his shoulders. "How much time did you give him to cover it up? A few hours? Did you only just come from there?"

Mikaeus's jaw twitched. Rorian knew him well enough to read it. "You say you want to help me," Rorian mocked, reaching for words as his weapon when nothing else was in reach. "Yet you have failed me at every turn. You have failed all of us. How many times did our father's information reach you before your ears could catch the truth? How many times did you let your findings confirm his bias instead of seeing the picture for yourself?"

"Rory," Mikaeus said in a strained tone, "if you do not work through this bewitchment, father will try you for treason. If you cannot be pulled back into reason you may lose your *life*, do you understand that?"

Options lay between them for Rorian. He knew them well. He could play along, go back into his shell of ignorance and live to see another day. Live to see Eheren again, escape at his first chance and run for the hills, taking her with him somewhere far away. Somewhere they could be together, free of his father's rule.

If he even made it that far. If Mikaeus did not keep eyes on him at all times, waiting for him to return to the witch to take her again. This time there would be no cell for her to press her back against, only the quick kiss of a blade to her beautiful neck.

So Rorian chose the second option. The one where he kept her safe. Where he faced the dawn a dead man, but one that did not waiver. Where he could buy time to bring the truth to his brothers, to give those children and all other witches a chance at life, even at the cost of his own.

"The only one bewitched is you," he growled, "by the lies of our father. Mother would be ashamed to see the man you've become, Mikaeus, to know the atrocities we've committed in our mother's name. No more." He leaned back in the chair, turning to the window and the woods far beyond. To Eheren. "Not for me."

Mikaeus had closed his eyes. His shoulders seemed heavier, decision settling upon him.

"If words can no longer reach you," he said, opening his eyes once more, glazed over for the work in hand, "then we will try other methods of getting you back."

"Do your worst," Rorian challenged.

He had.

Rorian gave them nothing on Eheren. They'd wanted to know where she was, how she'd found him and worked her magic into him. He talked instead about all the inconsistencies of their father's lies, gave them the truth as best he understood it about witches kept in the cells his father now hid and laid all on the table for Mikaeus to see, even if he refused to.

He never gave them her name. Her name was not for the likes of men, she'd told him their first meeting. He'd earned it, day by day, with love and patience.

He would not give it up in pain.

When it was clear he would not reveal what they wanted, Mikaeus simply snapped his fingers, calling his men to him. Hours had passed. Rorian was slumped in the chair, his stomach and ribs aching from the beating he'd endured, one eye almost swollen shut. The inside of his mouth was a canvas of cuts where fists had pushed his teeth into the flesh. Blood splattered the carpet in small drops, all of it his. He'd not fought back against the onslaught, only using his voice and words.

The door had opened, and he'd looked up blearily to Mikaeus greeting his father in the hall.

"Well?" Was all Fallon asked.

Mikaeus had shaken his head.

And then the door had closed, leaving him in darkness.

Rorian had pulled himself to the bed, collapsing into its familiar embrace. With his good eye he'd looked out to the woods, wishing he could see her just one more time.

They'd come for him at dawn. Six of his father's men, Jordan leading them. He couldn't have found the strength to fight even if he'd wanted to. Instead he'd pulled himself up, keeping his head held high.

"We have not found your witch, yet," his next eldest brother said, with no hint of emotion on his face. "Rest assured, though, we will in time."

Rorian chuckled, his chest unwinding from the spring of anxiety that had held him awake all night. "For your sake," he said, "pray you don't."

Thank you, he'd said with his eyes. Jordan couldn't meet his.

Then he'd been dragged to his feet, the irons on his wrists as heavy as his heart as they'd led him to the western wall.

King Fallon was waiting for them, Mikaeus at his side. A collection of the king's men gathered around the raised stone platform at the widest section of the wall, some to play the usual role of guards, others there on orders by their king to bear witness. There were a lot more present than usual. Clearly his father meant to make a point with this charade.

Rorian was led to the middle of the raised stone platform and brought to his knees with a swift kick. He gritted his teeth in determination not to give them the satisfaction of hearing his pain. A large man in a black cloak, the hood pulled up to obscure his face in the dim light, stood before him. To the side was his father, in equally dark clothes, and his brothers, Jordan joining his place beside Mikaeus.

"Prince Rorian Andreas Delafoy, youngest son of King Fallon Michael Delafoy, you stand trial today for crimes of a most heinous nature. For the high crime of treachery against the crown," the executioner boomed in a low baritone that carried far, "how does the accused plead?"

"Not guilty," Rorian tilted his chin back, turning his eyes to the king, "unlike my father."

"For consorting with witches and welcoming witchcraft into our city, how does the accused plead?"

"Guilty," he said, because he would never deny his love for Eheren.

Jordan looked shocked, as if someone had yanked the air from his lungs. Mikaeus only watched on grimly. His father was as impassive as stone.

"For the crimes of deception and spreading of falsehoods, how does the accused plead?"

"Not guilty," he said, "I have spoken no lies, and I will die for the truth today an innocent man."

The executioner paused, then looked to his king. "How does the crown find him on these charges?"

Fallon stepped toward, his hands clasped in front of him. His decorated black cape moved with the breeze. This was the one chance he had, the time when the king, above all els,e could pardon his crimes. The king's word was law, even if he was the one who set this in motion to start.

Jordan looked at his father's back, as if silently begging him to reconsider. Mikaeus studied Rorian, his eyes narrowed into inquisitive slits. Neither spoke in his favor.

They were too afraid to join him.

"The crown finds Prince Rorian Andreas Delafoy, youngest prince of the Fallon line, guilty of all charges," their father declared, "his sentence will not be lenient for his title nor blood. He has been determined to be beyond saving, his mind too far gone in the grips of a bewitchment. His sentence," he handed out, "is death."

His father had moved in such a way that his view of his eldest brother was blocked, so Rorian met the eyes of Jordan and held them.

Know that I am innocent, he begged him silently, *keep her out of his hands when I'm gone.*

Spare those children's lives.

His father began to lay out his tale of a witch who stole into the castle in an attempt to kill his line and instead was stopped by twelve *good men,* all slain dead. He continued to say how this witch had worked her magic on Rorian, how she'd poisoned him against his own country and family, and how there was no return. He was long winded, embellishing details and focused on the evil creature that had captivated his poor son, and how this sickness must not spread, how she must be found and stopped.

"Today I lose a son," his voice cracked, as if holding himself together. "Tomorrow, her head will roll beside him."

"Tomorrow," Rorian spoke up for the first time since the long winded speech had begun, "dawn will rise, and your hands will still be stained with the blood of your own son you have killed to keep your sins ongoing. May the Ley never take you home, and may your gods never hear your prayers, as they have turned away from those whose deaths you've wrought in malice."

His father was not impressed, a scowl slipping over his features before he could school them again. "You speak to me of the Ley, a witch's belief?" He shook his head. "My son is already dead."

It shouldn't have hurt. But it did. Being so harshly thrown aside by his father, a man he had revered until only a few short weeks before? It was like the knife was already in his chest.

The executioner stepped forward, ready to ask the next question in his practiced ritual, but Fallon shook his head.

"No," said the King, holding a hand in front of the man. "I will carry out this deed myself. He was my son."

Rage rang in Rorian's ears. To all others he may seem a strong leader in the face of a tragic decision, but he knew it was not duty that had called him to take over. *This* was personal.

Rorian had seen through his ploy, and for it he would pay with his life.

Fallon took the executioner's place, his face steady and regal. Rorian looked up from his place on his knees, the iron shackles behind him, calculating any way that he could fight out of this. He found none. It was futile.

This truly would be his end.

"How will you face your sentence?" The King asked.

"By sword," he called loud enough for everyone to hear, "may you remember the feeling of your blade striking me dead to keep your treachery alive. The price of your crusade will be my head, severed by your hand."

He glared at his father in challenge, and for a moment, only the briefest of ones, he saw something like regret flicker there. Then it was gone, replaced with grim determination.

Justification.

"Jordan," his father ordered, holding out his hand, "my blade."

Jordan hesitated, then stepped forward, a long, dark box in his hands. The King unleashed the clasps, revealing a long steel sword Rorian had seen only a handful of times. The steel blade glowed in the light of the braziers.

It wasn't the normal sword reserved for executions. This one was built for the death of magical beings, a stark comment on how low the king viewed him.

"Any last words?" He asked in tradition.

Rorian raised his head, looking at his father but speaking to his brothers, Eheren's words on his lips.

"The king's word may be law," he did not waiver, "but law is not truth."

Fallon did not wait beyond the final word. The King raised his sword high, readying to swing downwards, pausing only to breathe.

Rorian closed his eyes.

Eheren, his last thought was of her.

Hell burst forth from the stairwell. With a scream akin to a war cry, Heartless leapt onto the platform's far edge, capturing the attention of every man there. Rorian opened his eyes and turned not to the horse, but the crushingly familiar woman astride him.

Eheren. His witch.

Her black untamed hair flew away from her like smoke, the irises in her eyes swimming with iridescence from the power she held inside her. She'd been gathering it in her ribcage the entire frenzied ride there, growing it larger and winding it tighter until it spilled away, her mouth metallic with the taste. The eyes that turned on the men who meant to do Rorian harm shimmered silver like a demon's.

The witch burned with magic so thick it hurt to look upon her. It crawled across her skin, screaming as she tore it from the Ley with her teeth and twisted it into her bidding. An electric crackle filled the air, raising the hair on every man's neck just as sure as their fear did.

And oh, how they *feared* her. She could scent it on them, ripe and intoxicating, a rightness in the world to offset the wrongness she'd twisted her worldly gifts into. It was a delicate balancing act, and all it would take was one push before the roar in her ears lashed into the world.

She didn't have to wait long.

"Kill the witch!" The king roared, turning away from Rorian for only a second to command his men, "I want her head!"

Heartless screamed beneath her when weapons of cold steel turned to them, his desire for blood and battle rising to his cold, black eyes. Eheren stood fully on his back, letting the men witness the long black tunic she wore, the cape that floated behind her like a shadow, let them get an eyeful of her indigo skin and the expression of pure determination on her face.

She raised one arm straight out, pointing a single, delicate finger their way.

"Anyone who touches him," she promised, her voice amplified on the stones, "will meet death today."

Rorian's eyes were wide, wet with tears not meant for himself. "Eheren," he breathed, her name like a prayer.

"Leave the prince," ordered their king once more, "and kill that witch!"

So be it.

As soon as the first man moved towards them, Eheren let Heartless charge. The stallion went straight into their ranks heedless of their weapons, his teeth bared, his massive heft pushing a multitude down and his hooves crushing at least one man's leg. His screams were the first, but not the last. Someone took a swing at her, having rounded the horse and avoided his trampling charge, and it was the last mistake he made.

Eheren had never learned how to fight, she'd once told the prince, but she'd learned how to kill.

The magic of the Ley swelled within her, pulling from all directions, and she channeled it from the ground through the feet of the man. In one moment there stood a soldier, and the next there was a pyre of white flame, raw magic burning so hot within him his sword melted in his hands until all that remained was a black smudge on the ground. The next man was already swinging, not having caught up to the first's fate, and from her chest she lashed out a whip of the same raw magic for the same results.

Someone shouted a prayer, and she yanked the words from his throat, closing her hand in a fist and burning her magic underneath his tongue. He fell to the ground, eyes vacant, half his neck removed for his effort.

It was chaos worse than any battlefield. Rorian had wasted no time taking advantage of it, kicking his leg up to knock free the sword from his father's grip and rolling away. He was still bound by irons, ones he stepped over to bring before him, his body screaming with protests from the beating he'd taken the night before. Fallon cried out, turning for his sword, buying him precious moments to escape the immediate danger his father possessed.

Some men ran into battle and others away from the rampaging horse and witch, those smart enough to live another day fled for their lives, although Heartless blocked their exit to the stairs. Eheren leapt down, dropping low beneath a swinging blade and bringing up her hands to grab the man's leg, cleaving his body in half with another whip of the Ley.

"Rorian!" His father boomed, picking up his sword to follow the prince who fled for distance.

A guard came at him, another sword raised, but Rorian had trained with these very men for years. He threw himself beneath the reach of his weapon and shoved his shoulder into the man's stomach, knocking him down and leaving him behind as an obstacle.

His father found him again, leaping over the man to advance, swinging his blade down from another high arc, aiming for his shoulder and torso.

Rorian swiveled to face him and held his hands up, tightening the short chain between them. The sword smashed through them, the effort throwing the king off balance so the blow managed a shallow slash in the space above Rorian's eye, spilling blood into his vision but leaving him alive and free. He cried out at the pain, both the cut and the horrible feeling of the metal cuffs digging into his wrist when they'd been separated.

Rorian fell back, kicking out with his foot, gaining him a few feet of distance before Heartless, frenzied with bloodlust, barreled between them, creating a wall between them. Rorian scrambled to his feet again and ran for it, looking around desperately for his witch in the chaos.

She was still in the thick of it, the brutality of her kills spilling guts and burns across the stone. Needless death filled the platform around Jordan, who had lost line of sight on both his brothers. Alarm bells rang in his head, years of experience calculating their odds. He was a trained soldier and knew that when facing an enemy, especially a witch, you never took your eyes off of them.

Yet all he'd seen was good men meeting their death.

"Fall back!" He ordered, and many were happy to oblige, racing for the wall or stairs only to find Heartless there, mowing them down. He crushed skulls beneath his massive hooves, bit through cloth and into flesh, and ignored any blow that landed on him as if a harmless brush of grass. Guards scattered, yet still a few advanced on the witch, slipping in the gore. A young soldier he'd known to have recently joined his father's men raced in headstrong, ignoring his order altogether.

"No!" Jordan shouted, but the king's men did not heel. The man's sword swung in a perfect arc, a clean swing aimed at her neck, but never connected. At the back end of his swing a weight tipped his blade downwards and he turned his head from where the witch had stood a moment before.

Balancing on the flat plane of his sword with the pads of her toes Eheren moved like an asp, striking his face with an open palm. The man screamed when she unleashed the pulse of magic, his eyes melting into his head, his skull exploding from the other side. She danced off the blade before it could fall, gone before the corpse hit his knees on the stone.

Jordan had seen magic before, wielded countless ways, but never *this*. There was no spellwork here, just a brutal calling of power released through anyone who got too close.

"Rorian!" She called out, and Jordan saw him at last.

His younger brother was back in the middle of the platform, chasing around Heartless and into their line of sight. Blood and tears of relief stained his face, the first thing Jordan noted.

The second was the look of pure, unfiltered love for the witch who'd come for him. Something new and wonderful, a light he'd never seen him wear. Even in the middle of a slaughter this horrible, surrounded by death and destruction, he was glowing with it, like a man coming home after months at war.

Jordan turned to where his father strode for his younger brother, murder in his eyes. He'd seen that look of rage and blood-lust before on the faces of lesser men, but never him. And never at one of the princes.

Anyone who touches him will meet death today.

He needed to slay the monster cutting down his father's men. He needed to keep his family safe. He was a warrior, a general, a man of men who had taken pride in a lifetime of ridding the world of all who could harm his family, his kingdom.

But right now it wasn't the witch who looked to hurt them.

"Rorian!" His father called once more, turning his brother's warrior instinct from the frightening woman for only a second.

Without thought of how damned this would make him, if he'd become tomorrow's traitor, he was running, lunging around guards and soldiers until his father's blade that aimed for his brother's head instead met his.

They clashed together in strength, Fallon no frail man, until Jordan shoved him away at the cost of being pushed back against his brother.

Rorian's eyes were wide. Jordan, a man of honor, *Jordan*, who'd done their father's bidding in perfect order for most of his life, had disobeyed the king for him. Stepped before his sword and saved his life.

"Why?" he demanded, but Jordan was already moving, refusing to take his eyes off the king, regaining his footing after the shock of it.

"Because someone once told me that if I did my damn job right, you politicians would never see battle," he shouted over his shoulder, then swallowed hard before adding "and because you're my little brother."

"Jordan," he cried, "he'll kill you for this!"

"Neither of us are dying today," Jordan promised. "Go! Get to your witch!"

"Jordan–"

"*I said go!*" The older man roared, and for once in his life Rorian listened to his brother.

He was shaky on his feet, one eye closed to the blood pouring from his face wound, and the moment he sprinted away his father tracked it, attempting to intercept him and relieve his body of its head, but Jordan was right there to intercept again.

"Have you gone mad?!" The king roared at Jordan, turning his rage upon him.

"Have you?" He shouted back, fixing his stance yet refusing to strike his father unless provoked. "He's your son! I am too! Can't you see how he looks for her? What she's done for him? You'd kill him for falling in love?"

"I'd kill anyone," he snarled, "lowly enough to bed a witch."

And then it was not Jordan's sword that came for him, but another. The king parried it, both of them whirling to find Mikaeus beside them, his longsword turned on their father too.

"Is Mother on that list, then?" The normally impassive man shook with rage, and the shock of his words hit Jordan like a fist.

The King narrowed his eyes. "So you knew," he hissed.

"Knew what?" Jordan held his ground, unsure.

"I knew she was happy," the eldest brother explained with ice in his tone, "and that happiness cost her her life. I was foolish enough to believe you when you said she'd been bewitched, coerced and tricked until he took her life."

"Knew *what?*" Jordan insisted.

The king and Mikaeus were both leaning into their blades, neither willing to step back from this fight.

"Our mother was not slain by a witch, was she?" Mikaeus demanded of his father as much as he answered Jordan, "She met someone new, fell in love with him. You found out about her infidelity, and you let an innocent man die for it!"

"What?" Jordan whirled on his father, his sword faltering.

"I didn't believe it until I saw the truth of Rorian's words," Mikaeus snarled, his blade tip flicking.

"The man you claimed killed her, his hands were free of stain. With every life taken today, her's has only grown," he motioned with his head to the witch Rorian ran for, to the deep marks that had now climbed upwards to her shoulders.

"How easy it would be to blame him for your crime of passion, to turn that treachery outwards and start a needless war."

"No," Jordan stumbled over the word, "he couldn't, he wouldn't..." but he was unsure, his heart rolling in pain at the possibility.

"You don't know him like I do," Mikaeus growled, circling their father, his sword never wavering. "Do you continue to deny these claims, father?"

Fallon said nothing, following his son's steps. "Traitors, all of you," he spoke at last, keeping his footwork in time.

"Just like your mother."

Jordan was the first to move, an explosion of muscle and force. He screamed with the effort, his large steel blade raising over his head, tears threatening to steal his vision. Fallon pushed him away with ease, turning in time to block Mikaeus's next strike, a quick move with perfect form. The three of them danced together in a whirl of steel, their blades forged to slay witches now turned against their fellow men.

Their father.

His sons.

One last man stood against Rorian when he ran, the dark hooded executioner quick to rise from the shadows at the edge of the platform. A long dagger shone in his hand. Rorian lunged away, barely escaping its reach, only for blood to explode from what was once the executioner's body, the cape slumping in a formless heap where Eheren had ripped out his chest.

Shock filled Rorian at the sight, and the blood that now coated him, and then he was moving again, not caring about the death around him, his eyes for one person alone.

They met in the middle, Rorian flinging his arms around her and Eheren pulling him close, closing her eyes to the chaos of Heartless's onslaught and the clamor of sword against sword.

"Eheren," he cried against her, wiping the blood off her shoulder. "Your arms," he gasped, seeing the indigo stain had crawled up nearly to her neck.

"Never mind that," she pulled his face to hers, kissing him like her life depended on it.

He returned the kiss, lost in the feeling of it all, the emotions at facing his death, and the thought of never seeing her again overwhelming him at last..

She pulled away to return her focus to the world around them, but he was laughing, still gripping her arms.

"Remind me never to piss you off," he choked, "by the gods, Eheren, I've never seen anything like what you've done–"

"It's not over yet," she warned him, and he turned to look at his brothers facing off against his father.

Mikaeus had taken a deep slash across his sword arm's bicep, his blade transferred to his off-hand. Jordan was taking the lead to cover him, pushing into his father's range more, taking dangerous risks to keep him away from Mikaeus.

"No," Rorian choked, looking back at Eheren.

She was exhausted, he could tell, the strain of the magic she'd abused written on the tight lines of her face. She had done so much for him, killed so many to keep him alive... but those were his brothers who now faced death.

For him.

"Stay here," he ordered, turning to a man who sat cowering against the nearby wall, his head over his hands.

"You!" he barked, causing the man to cry out. "Your sword, give it to me."

"Rorian," the witch tried to argue, but his eyes were fire and determination.

"This ends today," he said to her, "and I won't allow you to stain yourself any more for my sake."

"Don't you dare–" she began, but he left her, striding over to take the man's sword himself. The guard made a bawling sound, hiding away from the witch behind him.

"I love you," he told Eheren, the one thing he'd regretted he may never say again, and then he was off, eating the distance between him and his father in seconds.

"Rorian!" she called, going to race after him only for her leg to give way, the Ley receding from her like a wounded animal.

"Damnit," she swore, pushing herself back up, locked in a struggle for control. "Rorian!"

Jordan took a swipe across his chest, seconds later, blood spilling down his uniform and soaking the fabric. Mikaeus moved to parry the next swing only to lose his grip from a vicious blow, faltering back.

"She was *mine,*" the king sneered, still locked in on their fight.

Jordan took a step back with the next attack, then another, solidly on the offensive.

"Promised to me, *bound* to me, and that bastard played with what he didn't own. You think I killed your mother out of malice? It was *she* who jumped on my sword to save his life!"

Jordan blocked twice again, gritting his teeth in pain from the wound bleeding freely.

"Why?' He demanded, parrying another blow and barely escaping another that crossed his forearm, drawing another thin line of pain.

Fallon's face was twisted in anger, lost in the moment he'd killed their mother.

"His blood wasn't enough," he swung again, grazing the skin from his son's knuckles, "he had to pay for taking her from me, they *all* did!"

"You've gone mad!" Jordan swung at his blade hand, missing and paying for it dearly. His father kicked out with his boot, landing a blow in the fresh line across his chest. Jordan screamed with the pain, his sword clattering to the ground where his muscles faltered.

"Stop!" Mikaeus shouted, but their father did not.

"I am *king,*" Fallon shouted down at his sons, blood lust in his eyes, "I am *infallible!*"

His sword came down for his opponent, a blow that would sink deep into his throat and chest, his favorite finishing move. Rorian had seen it a thousand times, practiced against it, studied every move again and again like the trade ledgers he'd poured himself into.

He stepped low, cutting his sword up to move the slash wide, paying for it with a deep cut across his shoulder he ignored. With his own roar of challenge he stepped into his father's now wide-open stance, headbutting him as hard as he could. The crunch of bones met his ears and shook through his head, a white hot splitting pain accompanying it.

Fallon fell backwards, sword still in hand, but Rorian didn't need to see through the agony. Jordan and Mikaeus may have been the fighters in his family, but he was not without countless hours of study himself. He brought his blade down in a stabbing move directly into his father's sword arm, cutting straight through the flesh between his bones.

Fallon screamed while Rorian's sight returned to him, bringing his foot down on his father's bloodied wrist. Fallon's sword came free of his hand and Rorian dropped to grab it, wielding it under-handed while kneeling on his father's chest and pressing the blade against the soft flesh under his chin.

Fire burned within Rorian, his breathing heavy. Jordan rose to his feet behind him, Mikaeus struggling to stand at his side.

"You are a man," he heaved, pressing the sword in deeper when he tried to move. Red blood welled from the cut, his eyes wide in shock. "And all men are mortal. Care to test it?"

Rorian's eyes were cold, another feature he'd gained from his father.

"You've lost," he told him, his body shaking.

Not removing the sword from his father's throat he moved to stand. Eheren slipped beside him to put her arm around his waist, helping hold him aloft. His body screamed in agony and exhaustion, yet it wasn't time to rest.

"But," he continued, looking at the woman against his side, "your death is not mine to claim."

All eyes turned to the raven-haired witch, to the blood soaking her clothes and skin, a monster by her own right.

She beheld the man of her nightmares. The man who ordered the death of everyone she'd ever loved, who had caged her in the earth, surrounded her in death and despair. His eyes held pure hatred for her, but also a healthy dose of fear. Fear she drank in, the last of the Ley she held within her screaming for her to stop, at war with the call of revenge she was so rightly owed.

Rorian leaned into her, a silent grant of permission. It broke her in ways she couldn't quantify, for the man she loved so wholly to lay the life of his father in her hands.

"...I will not weld the Ley against such a creature," she said at last, her voice dark. "His stain will not marr my skin."

She released the last of the Ley within her, feeling its absence and the stone wall it placed between them. She did not know if it would ever heed her call again after today. If that was the price to pay to save Rorian's life, she thought, so be it. She loved magic with all her heart, but every other part was his. She'd make do..

Rorian nodded, not taking his eyes of his father.

"Your time as king is over," he proclaimed, loud enough for everyone left alive to hear. "You are a disgrace to the throne. You have admitted your crimes to all, shown your true hand. No one will come to your aid."

"Go to hell," Fallon spat blood at his feet, but Rorian did not care. "None of you are fit to rule! You don't have what it takes to keep this country safe, to do what needs done."

"One of us does."

Jordan was the first to kneel, laying his sword on the ground. "I am a general," he continued, his head bowed to his youngest brother, "not a king."

Mikaeus stood as a statue would, the blood of his men setting into his clothes. Rorian looked at him through his open eye, his chin high, even as Eheren had to hold him upright. Mikaeus had always been closest to their father, had even tortured Rorian on his word. The crown was his by birthright. He'd trained his entire life for it.

Rorian stared down his eldest brother, waiting.

"Our father is not yet dead," he spoke directly to Rorian, "yet he is no king. Nor am I."

Fallon began to scream obscenities at them all, the cries of a child who'd lost his favorite game. The look Mikaeus scalded the shrieking man with could have melted flesh from bone.

"I am not so bold a man as to face against a wild witch, nor the man foolish enough to have caught her affection. Long live the king," he turned his back, "I return to my men to spread the word of your rise and await your orders."

"Son," croaked the king through his blood. When his eldest did not stop, the croak turned into a wail. "Mikaeus!"

The eldest stopped walking long enough to turn over his shoulder to be heard. "It should have been you, not mother."

He left his parting words like a blow, disappearing down the wall and leaving his family behind.

Leaving Rorian a king, earned by battle rights.

Rorian did not look like a king. Nor did he feel like one. He felt hollow, beaten, tired. But Eheren's arms held him steady, and for what she'd done here today— what she'd done for *him*, at the cost of something very valuable to herself— he pretended he could be a king.

The eyes of his father's men all watched him. Those surviving, anyway. Those who had heeded Eheren's warning.

Any who touch him die here.

And all who survive shall live. And he will command them.

So command them he did.

"Blind him," ordered their new king, his eyes as unyielding as onyx when they turned upon his father, "and let his dungeons be his new home. Let him rot and fester in the dark until he craves his pit, and only then will we release him. Banishment from the light will be your punishment. Let him discover just how searing the irons of freedom can burn. Let him crave the nothingness he gave my wife."

Eheren stiffened against him, her wild eyes glowing with surprise. He did not stumble over the word.

Wife.

"I'd planned to ask you differently," he murmured to only her.

"We aren't married," she whispered back, too stunned to say anything else.

In spite of his pain, his injuries, the cavern in his heart from the treachery and crimes of his father, Rorian smiled.

"Yet."

The men did not hesitate. They'd witnessed it all themselves, heard his confession.

They picked his father up, a mess of swears and unbecoming pleas on deaf ears.

"You will regret this!" Fallon shouted, "Unhand me! I am your king! He is a boy, bewitched by a murderer! *Heed me!*"

None of them did. One man, someone Rorian knew to be friends with Jordan from their time in the training grounds, produced a small blade from his boot.

Fallon's eyes went wide. "No!" He shrieked, struggling in vain against the men who held him, "No!"

Rorian did not look away when they plucked out his eyes. He did not turn his ears away from his screams.

Neither did Eheren. Nor Jordan.

Then the fallen king was dragged away, across the field of blood to the stairs and down below, his cries of agony and rage following all the way.

"Hail King Rorian," someone shouted, the first of the few left standing.

"Hail!" they called out, placing their hand to their chest, their swords to the ground.

If only everyone would fall in line so easily. It would be a long road to a clean rule, even once word of the day spread by Mikaeus's connections.

At last Rorian leaned his full weight into her, collapsing. Eheren hugged him close, falling down with him to their knees. He buried his face in her neck, his hand tangling with the blood saturated mess her hair had become.

"I'll need to get you another cloak," he murmured, feeling the fabric between his fingers. "This one is absolutely ruined."

Tears welled in her eyes as she hugged him tightly, kissing his cheek.

"You absolute fool," she cried against him. "I couldn't care less about a cloak, only you."

"I'm positively fine," he lied, resting his forehead against her. "The cloak not so much."

Eheren's eyes snapped up to the sound of approaching footfall, attempting to will magic to her on instinct. The Ley sobbed in her ears, no longer in Rorian's name but in its own for what she'd twisted it into.

It did not come.

At the sight of her eyes Jordan froze, moving again in slow, obvious motions to kneel beside his brother, a healthy distance from her reach.

"Rory," he asked, his eyes never leaving hers, "are you okay?"

"Gods," Rorian laughed, sniffling and turning in her arms to face his brother. "Are you?"

"No," he answered honestly. He knelt beside them, touching the open wound on his chest. "I don't think any of us are."

"Love," Rorian said to Eheren, "this is my middle brother, Jordan. When I was imprisoned by my father he led the hunt for you in the wrong direction. He saved your life, so stop glaring death at him, please."

Jordan managed a strained laugh.

"You were right," he told Rorian, "I'm glad we did not find her. That was... something," he landed on, meaning her slaughter to save his brother.

Eheren eyed him warily.

"You were the first to lay your sword down to him," she spoke, her clear inflection startling him, "and you stopped your father's sword from finding his neck."

"Yes he did," Rorian put a hand on her cheek, turning it to face his, "so, please, leave him be? I'm quite fond of him. Don't let him know," he whispered conspiratorially, "but he's my favorite brother."

"I heard that," Jordan snorted.

"Damnit, you weren't supposed to," he joked back, smiling with him.

Eheren relaxed at last, offering the warrior a stiff nod. Jordan visibly relaxed, granting her a weak smile.

"So," he said, "shall we get cleaned up? We all look like, well, like we went through a war, and I have a feeling we won't get much time to breathe, soon enough."

Jordan reached out, touching Rorian's shoulder. "Kings aren't known for their downtime, especially new ones."

Rorian groaned.

"There will need to be a coronation," he began to count, "and we'll need to weed out any still loyal to our father–"

"More than that," Jordan interrupted, offering them both a large grin, "I believe I'm owed the story of how my *sister-in-law* came into your life, and what you've *really* been up to in those woods for months."

Rorian gave up, lying back against her chest. "Is it still too late to be beheaded?"

"I'm afraid so," Eheren stood, helping him up alongside his brother, who put his good arm under hers to support him. Rorian leaned against them both, trying not to moan with the various pains he'd gathered.

"Could I have your name?" Jordan asked Eheren, leading them back towards the stairs. Off to the side, two men tried to maintain their distance from Heartless while also guiding him back towards the stables, a venture she supposed might take all day, if they succeeded at all. He stamped his hooves and screeched any time they advanced too close.

"We'll see," Eheren answered him, "but a warm bath and good food might persuade me."

"Oh," Rorian cracked a smile, "our cook is going to *love* you."

"You haven't been passing along my compliments?" She asked, heading him down the stairs.

Rorian laughed, a genuine, bright sound that reassured Jordan this had all been worth it.

"My love, he may have seasoned it, but *I've* been the one cooking it."

"I've already shown you my gratitude plenty," she teased, grateful to have a moment more of his banter.

"Oh, just wait until my wounds are healed," he promised, "I'll accept *all* the gratitude you can give.'

"Gods, I'm going to regret this greatly," Jordan asked, "aren't I?"

"Be nice, I am your king," Rorian wheezed, his lungs complaining again with each step.

"Does he ever shut up?" Eheren asked his brother.

"Oh never," he promised.

"I guess I'll have to get used to it then," she smiled, taking things one step at a time, "since I've decided I'm to be his wife."

Rorian's face lit up like the sun, another laugh bouncing off the stairs around them. "Did you hear that, Jordan?" he asked. "She said yes!"

~ Chapter Fourteen ~

HOME

By the time they'd reached the doors to Rorian's chambers nearly a full day later, neither was sure which one was holding up the other. Eheren's burning pain had turned to a dull, crying ache in her body, and exhaustion from the whirlwind day settled deep. Rorian was not in a much better state, propping himself on the wall with one hand to open the door.

The darkness of very early morning greeted them, no candles lit within, the outlines of furniture only visible as silver lines from the moon's glow. He didn't bother to set any lights, only guided them both to the large bed in the second room before falling onto it with a groan of relief.

"I'll give you a tour tomorrow," his words came muffled through the blanket he was face-down upon, "I can't even remember the names for my furniture right now."

"I believe this is called a bed," She sat next to him, peeling the tunic she still wore from her body.

"If you insist."

"It's more like five of them set together." She'd never seen one quite so large, with four posts reaching up to the ceiling to hold a canopy up high, dark fabric curtains pulled back with ties.

"Plenty of room— pick a corner, any corner, and claim it."

She reached over to tug at his shirt, pulling it away with minimal help on his part. "I want whatever corner you're in."

Rorian cracked a smile, turning his head to face her. "Then pull me into your favorite."

They ended up right in the middle, entwined beneath the sheets like they'd done so so many nights before. It was much softer than her pile of blankets and furs, and smelled like perfumed soaps and him.

Eheren turned to him, caressing his face to reassure herself that he was here, and real, and alive. The bandage over his forehead had been hastily done, but held for the time being.

"I'm here," he said, understanding the look in her eyes. "All thanks to you."

"You're a king now," she breathed.

"And you a queen, soon enough."

Eheren had to credit him for his boldness.

"You still haven't properly asked me."

"I'll add it to my growing mountain of to-do's. Somewhere at the top, I promise."

She tilted her chin enough to look at her shoulder, at the indigo stain that now rose nearly to her collar.

"What good would I be as a queen? No one will accept me. I've killed too many of your men."

"I've already pardoned you. And they weren't *my* men, but my father's."

"Your country wages a war against my kind."

"A war built on lies," he reached up in turn to brush his fingers over her upper arm, a soft, loving touch. "Lies I plan to dismantle over time."

"They'll think you spellbound."

"Let me handle that."

She pursed her lips in frustration. "Rorian, this complicates things."

"We've always been complicated," he reminded her, "but now I am king, and the king's word is law."

"Then what is your law?" She pinched his cheek, "To never think anything through and push forward regardless on a fool's errand?"

"My law," Rorian shifted his weight, moving to hover above her with half his body, "is to dedicate every moment of my life to you. I will carve a place for us, for *you* in this world, with my own hands if I must, until my nails are gone and bleeding. You are not escaping me so easily, Witch."

Eheren was struck by his words, the weight of what he promised.

"I'm not running away," she offered her own vow, caressing his face. "I'm here with you, in any way you'll have me."

"As my wife?"

"I've already agreed to that."

His lips split into a grin. "I know," he said, "but I can't get enough of hearing it."

When he kissed her it felt like the first time all over again, submerged in the cool waters of the lake, in a world all their own. She let him deepen it, as desperate for him as he was her.

"When that sword was raised over my neck," he pulled away, swallowing with the admittance, "my last thought was you...and how I'd never get the chance to tell you that I loved you again. I plan to make up for that every day for the rest of our lives."

"I'll never grow sick of hearing it," she breathed, "although I retain the right to mercilessly tease you for it for all of time."

"For forever," he lay back beside her, nuzzling into her neck.

Eheren's eyes looked beyond him, to the tall window overlooking the forest they'd met. To the place she'd been so lost in for so long, waiting for him to crash into her life.

She held him tight, his breathing already evening out with sleep.

She held him tight, his breathing already evening out with sleep. She held him with the same tenderness, the same reverence she once held the Ley.

"Forever," she whispered into the night, finding peace at last.

The End

AUTHOR'S NOTE

This won't be the end of Ley's world. I cannot wait to bring Jordan's story to life very, very soon.

Find me online at **AuthorJennieElaine.com**

To all my readers who have made it this far, I cannot give you enough love for sticking through Rorian and Eheren's journey with me. This project was born out of a love for fantasy romance, the desire to create, and a simple avoidance of other writing and editing projects that were raking me through the coals.

Ley was a very welcome break and a book I absolutely would have picked up in high school and never put down. It's my first story aimed at teen audiences (I have *quite* the penchant for more mature stories,) and if even one younger reader loved this work, then I have succeeded as an author.

Writing any novel, whether it be 30,000 words or 150,000 takes an amazing village, and to that, I owe some credit.

As always, and as if the dedication wasn't enough, thank you a thousand times to Jenessa and Jan, who are not only my creative partners in all things writing, but put up with my daily antics as two amazing friends. Ley would not be half the story it was without you, and you know you have my whole heart for it.

To the newest member of my editing team, Victoria Wilson, I could scream your name from the rooftops for your hard work and wonderful personality. If I could keep you in a box and just have you edit everything I ever write, I'll be a NYT bestselling author in no time!

To Dakota, and his constant love and support of my arts, thank you to the moon and back.

And to the stellar team of Ink & Quill Press, you know I love you, but I'm so grateful to have a dedicated, kind publishing team behind my works. I have enjoyed every project I've had the pleasure of working on with you, and your offer to bring Ley to print warms my heart to no end.

MELDED, an illustrated dark fantasy and queer romance that will break your heart again and again

Gen is running from his fate—and love— but it's happening anyway.

He's rejected his responsibility to his island's temple to translate scrolls for Simon Holiday, a human ambassador with his own unavoidable past.

When Simon becomes the first human invited to the temple's most sacred ceremony, Gen might have a chance to balance duty with his growing feelings for him. Until another former apprentice, Jorel, seizes control of the temple's true power: Haliz Fundir, a tree-like being with the ability to meld people into one.

Jorel only needs one last piece of knowledge to unlock its dark strength— a secret only Gen holds. In a desperate move, Gen melds with Simon to escape.

Now sharing one body and mind, they must confront their pasts and survive on an island bent on their destruction.

With Jorel's followers, the last remaining human resistance, a deranged scientist, and monstrous creatures hunting them, time is running out before Haliz Fundir awakens and consumes them all. Gen and Simon are their last hope, with nowhere to run except inside their own minds.

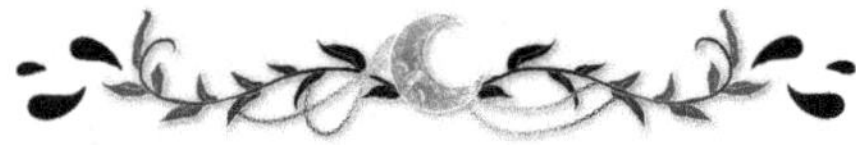

A collection of science fiction short stories featuring Jennie's contribution, BLACK ANGEL

A story of lunar cartels, love squandered, and debts come to collect

In a dilapidated trailer park on Luna our narrator finds the former lover of Donner Mayberry, the moon's most notorious drug cartel lord to ever rise from the craters.

As she weaves a story of their rise and her fall alongside the deadly drug Black Angel, it soon becomes clear that our narrator is there for more than just a story, and life, love, and debts all come to collect.

Follow the author at **AuthorJennieElaine.com** to never miss a release!